The Cockroach
Chronicles

The Cockroach Chronicles

BOOK ONE: The Secret of The Loch

DR. SUSAN PHIBBS CECIL

The Cockroach Chronicles
Book One: The Secret of The Loch

Copyright © 2013 by Dr. Susan Phibbs Cecil
Illustrations Copyright © 2013 by Dr. Susan Phibbs Cecil

Publisher
CC Publishing Group

Notice of Rights

Interior Design: Kathy Besthorn, aLightGoesOn, Inc.
Cover Illustration: Peter Dorman Johnson, irlson02@gmail.com
Cover Design: Kathy Besthorn, aLightGoesOn, Inc.

ISBN – 978-1-4947-6151-6

1st Edition, December 2013
Printed and bound in the United States of America

FOR ALL YOU BANDITS ON YOUR QUEST FOR
LOVE, FAITH, AND TRUTH

TABLE OF CONTENTS

Chapter One   THE HEIRESS

Sloane woke up screaming. Sloane always woke up screaming. When she realized that no one heard her and no one cared she screamed again. She opened her eyes to a room that was a fantasy of wealth and taste. Taupe linens, solid gold picture frames, crystal chandeliers, heavy fabrics crusted with beads, antique etchings, the room was in a word- magnificent. Her canopy bed was enormous. She had to have a stool in order to climb into it. She often thought of "The Princess and the Pea". There could have been a dead wallaby under Sloane's mattress and she couldn't have felt it. Every morning when she stopped screaming, she licked the surfaces of the room with her eyes. Her favorite object was a huge floor mirror framed in branches. She had designed the mirror and insisted no living trees be cut to make it. The branches were cast in sterling and drizzled with eighteen carat gold. She slid off the bed and stood naked in front of the mirror. She was as beautiful as the room in which she stood. She was very tiny. Her dark wavy hair fell in a cascade to her shoulders. She was slender but finely muscled. She knew she was beautiful. She had been beautiful for a long time. At that moment, a huge black cockroach dropped out of her hair onto her shoulder. She smiled and said," Well, good morning and how is my fine Madagascar Hissing Cockroach?" The cockroach hissed.

There was a new riding outfit draped over the back of a chair. Obviously a maid had put it there in the night, because it wasn't there when Sloane went to sleep. It "creeped" Sloane out to have people in her room when she was sleeping but ever since they found the pills hidden away among her underwear, her Mother had insisted that the door to her room never be locked. Well, Sloane had bested them at their own game. In her unending hours of reading, she had discovered that the ancient Chinese committed suicide by eating a pound of salt. "Death by Dorito"- Sloane loved it. She stored the information away in the only private thing she had, her brain. All of Sloane's clothes were tailor made so the outfit was an exact fit. The boots were buttery soft leather. The outline of her toes could be seen through the tops. The pants were like a second skin. The jacket was set off by a lacy scarf tied at the throat. Sloane knew what this meant and sure enough, as she turned to the window, a white unicorn stuck his head in and looked at her. The unicorn was so fabulous that Sloane laughed right out loud. She could almost believe for a minute that he was real. He was real, of course. He was a real white stallion wearing a real unicorn headdress. The headdress was studded with crystals. There were cutouts for his eyes and it tied under his massive jaw. The horn was a natural shell. Tiny crystals had been brushed onto the horse's eye lashes and into its mane. Sloane knew what this meant. Mother would not be here with her today. If she even wanted to talk to her, Sloane would have to make the call. So she did.

"Mom, yes, he's here with me. He's sticking his head through the window. Yes, he's so wonderful. What, I can't hear you? You're in a hot air balloon? In Cappadocia? Duh, Mom, I know it's in Turkey. I've been there, remember? No I wasn't being rude and no, I don't need to speak to Neville. Thanks, Mom and Mom, I love…"

Sloane looked down at the phone in her hand. She had lost the connection. Sloane carefully set her pet cockroach down on a pile of amethysts that her mother had the maids sprinkle across the top of her dresser. She looked at her cockroach, "Don't worry. I don't love you less now that I have a horse. Every heiress needs a horse and a cockroach."

Sloane put her riding costume on as the horse watched from the window. He knew what that meant; they were going for a ride. He whinnied. Their first ride was a wild dance of two free young spirits. There were no adults around to warn her against riding the horse bareback so she sprang onto his back, bent low over his shoulders, twined her hands in his mane and set him loose. She was absolutely fearless. After what seemed like miles, Sloane slowed him to a walk. He had known immediately on seeing her to whom he belonged. It was love on sight. She led him into a shallow creek and slid off his back. She unfastened the unicorn headpiece and he tossed his head, glad to be rid of it. Then she began to carefully comb the crystals out of his mane with her fingers. On a whim, she took off her clothes and let them fall in the mud at the edge of the creek. Then she began the long walk home. The au pair watched from the window and from a distance it looked like the horse had tears in his eyes. Even a horse could feel the loneliness of a motherless child.

Back at the chateau, Sloane remembered that her Grandmother had sent her a present.

Sloane and her Grandmother shared a love for strange and ugly little things. The hissing cockroach was a gift from her Grandmother. She didn't see her package anywhere. Ah, there it was on the fur rug. The maids must not have seen it or they might have thrown it out. It surely was ugly. It was wrapped in brown paper that looked like it had been recycled more than once. Zebra patterned duct tape was wound randomly all over it and the corner actually had a tire tread across it. It was a book and when Sloane opened it, a note from her Grandmother fell out. "Happy Birthday Sloane, I wish I could be there with you and your Mom to celebrate this special occasion. I know you're having fun together. I have included two tickets for Scotland as I'm sure you will want to go after you read your book. XOXO, Grandmother" Sloane tore one of the tickets in half and saved it for a bookmark and the other one she pushed deep into the pocket of her jeans.

Chapter Two   THE MONSTER

Nessie woke up screaming. As soon as she heard the sound, she abruptly stopped. The last thing she needed was to draw attention to herself. She had found a ledge under an overhang. It was a perfect haven. She was safe from the sharks and close to the Plesiosaur mating grounds. Rays of sunshine slashed down through the water. It would have been perfect except for the loneliness. Her loneliness was as vast as the oceans. Nessie was a gentle animal, wanting nothing more than to swim through the earth's waters, eat fish and be with her own kind. It was what her species had done for sixty five million years. Within her lifetime, she had seen her fellow creatures at sea, in the lochs, at the mating grounds-dozens upon dozens of them. And how they rolled and played and danced in the water together. These animals were as much like their primeval ancestors as a modern human was like an ancient knuckle-walking ape. Only the smartest, the most physically superb of her kind survived and she was one of these. For months, she had been feeling a strange anxiety. Her body was noticeably bigger and she had a huge appetite. She had been driven by instinct to find a safe nest. She had only seen one birth in her entire life because the mothers usually secreted themselves away to protect themselves and their newborns. A delivery was especially dangerous. The small head and long neck of the newborn was easily pushed from the mother's body but the body of the baby was much larger and if the mother did not have the strength to force the bulk of the body out, she and the baby would die. It occurred to Nessie that she might have a baby inside her. She waited.

Chapter Three   THE CRYPTID

Since Sloane's ticket was for Scotland she knew what that meant - the Loch Ness monster.

And there she was on page 78. Sloane began to read first about the loch. She read page after page of facts. At the top of page seventy she abruptly stopped. She knew all she needed to know. The loch was flat, deep, dark and cold. Strangely her book noted that the loch would hold the bodies of seven billion dead people. A voice, whether hers or not, spoke inside her mind.

"Others have used facts and science and they have not found what you seek. Open your heart to your fellow creature and you may be deemed worthy."

The wonder of it, the joy of it was intoxicating to Sloane. She wouldn't even care if nobody ever knew that she had confirmed the existence of the monster. She just wanted to KNOW.

She opened her book again to study the pictures of Nessie. She fell asleep that night with the picture of Nessie lying over her heart.

Sloane packed light for her trip. She only took her laptop, and her IPad. She wanted to read Barrie, Robert Louis Stephenson and several recent scientific articles by the 2012 winner of the Nobel Prize – John Gurdon. Sloane smiled to herself because hardly anyone knew who Gurdon was. She thought he needed a better publicist.

The flight to Edinburgh was short and Sloane passed the time by thinking of all she would get to see and do in Scotland. She was most excited by her search for Nessie but she was also eager to see Dolly at the National Museum.

Chapter Four   THE SMURF QUEEN

Edinburgh castle is squat and mean and real looking. In the early morning, the fog hangs so low, the castle can't be seen. And when the fog burns off, the castle seems more oppressive than before. It is possibly the oldest castle in the British Isles. Its walls have only been breached twice and both times, the vanquishers were the Scots themselves. They were retaking their royal castle from the British.

 Sloane stood in the room where the royal jewels were displayed. She stood and quietly admired the ruby ring. She felt someone watching her, but when she looked around, no one was there. The room was very small and strangely dim. There, she felt it again. This time she saw someone's back as the person slipped away through the door. Oddly, the person wore an old-fashioned cape with the hood pulled forward. Sloane hurried after the person but it was too late. There was no one there. Sloane stood alone on the castle parapet.

Next morning, Sloane was the first person through the arch into the castle. Last night in her room, she had checked the map of the castle grounds on the internet just to reassure herself that she had not seen a ghost. She was not reassured.

She chose to go back to the Jewel Room. This time she hung back in a corner to see what might happen. The cloaked person stepped into the room. Sloane stepped forward and put her hand on the person's arm. At least, the arm was solid. The person jumped and scurried out but Sloane was quicker this time. She ran out the entrance and circled around to confront the person. What she saw froze her heart. The person was a young girl and in her haste her hood had slipped back off of her face. She was blue.

"Are you a demon?" Sloane stammered.

"Jesus, Are you dead?"

"No, I am an American. I am Sarah Trimbath from Kentucky and you shouldn't take the Lord's name in vain."

"I am Sloane Renee Gleeson from Kansas and I wasn't blaspheming," said Sloane under her breath.

"Oh, it's makeup. You must be here for the Royal Edinburgh Tattoo. What a beautiful costume".

"This is not a costume. These are my real clothes. This is my real color. And I am here to help you. I have seen someone following you"

"Yes, that would have been you", snipped Sloane.

'I think they intend to kill you."

The best response Sloane could stammer out was "Oh."

A small boy came running up to Sarah. He was yelling, "Mom, mom, look, a smurf, I didn't know they had Smurfs in Scotland."

He looked up into Sarah's face and said, "You're so pretty, you must be the queen Smurf."

"Why, yes I am."

And Sarah bent down and kissed the little boy on the cheek.

"I knew it. I knew it. A smurf."

The little boy danced a jig and clapped his hands in delight. The mother had reached the boy by then and she quickly stepped between the boy and Sarah. As she pulled him away, she looked back at Sarah as though she might have AIDS.

Sloane and Sarah immediately became friends as often happens when people are lonely.

Sarah explained to Sloane about her coloring, "It's genetic. The condition is called, Methemoglobinemia. It's very rare. I am a descendent of the Fugates from Troublesome Creek. Our Kentucky people have been blue for one hundred and sixty two years. We are healthy and some of us have lived to be eighty or ninety years old. We have high concentrations of methemoglobin in our blood. In the 1960's a doctor discovered that we lack the enzyme diasphorase. He was actually able to turn blue people pink by injecting them with methylene blue. The color change happens in minutes. The doctor gave the blue people a daily pill to maintain their new color."

"Will you have blue children?" Sloane was intrigued by Sarah's condition.

"Our skin color is recessive, so the only way my children would be blue is if I marry someone who has the gene."

"Why are you blue if you can take a pill and turn pink?"

"My mother believes that God intended us to be blue and therefore we should honor his choice. Besides, we have no money for such things. What if the pills harmed us in some unknown way?"

"Does it make you uncomfortable for people to stare at you? Are they rude?"

"Yes, people are rude. They are rude to people who are different from themselves, so they are especially rude to me. I think they are afraid. They think that I might have a contagious disease. Their fears are not illogical. Do you think I am ugly, Sloane?"

"No, I think you are like a genie or a goddess."

"Really, you really mean it? You're not just saying that to make me feel better?"

"I have been known to lie on rare occasion but I am not lying to you." Sloane looked very earnestly at Sarah and placing a hand on each side of her blue face said, "Sarah Trimbath, I think you are beautiful."

Chapter Five   DOLLY DEAREST

Edinburgh was the place where Dolly was cloned. Dolly was named after the American country singer, Dolly Parton. She was created from a breast cell of an adult sheep. The process was no less extraordinary than the possible existence of a prehistoric reptile. In fact, the creation of a living animal that did not result from the combination of genetic material from a male and a female of its own species seemed Frankenstein-like. Sloane had read that John Gurdon developed the two step process of "nuclear transfer" necessary for cloning. First, he removed the nucleus from an unfertilized frog cell. Then, he put the nucleus from a frog gut cell back into the cell. After a time the newly constructed cells matured into tadpoles. GURDON HAD CLONED LIVING CREATURES FROM ADULT CELLS. Cloned tadpoles do not mature into frogs. To create Dolly, a scientist combined the cells of a Scottish Blackface sheep and a Finn Dorset sheep. The cell was given a jolt of electricity, just like the Frankenstein monster. The electricity causes the nucleus to fuse with the contents of the new cell and to begin to divide. CELL DIVISION IS LIFE!! The process was repeated 276 times before the cell which had been put into a Blackface sheep resulted in the birth of Dolly, a Whiteface sheep. DNA analysis proved that Dolly was the result of a nuclear transfer. Dolly seemed normal in every way except that at a young age she developed conditions of old age. She became so ill that she was put to sleep. Before Dolly died she gave birth to lambs that are alive today. She was stuffed and put on display at the National Scottish Museum. Sloane and Sarah stood in front of the stuffed sheep and marveled. Sloane knew why there were maturation problems with cloning. The scientists were using old cells. She didn't bother to share her insight into the obvious. After all, she was a mere child. Sloane turned to Sarah and said,

"Have you heard that scientists in New Zealand have been given permission to put human DNA into sheep, goats, and cattle?"

"I beg your pardon?"

"Have you heard that scientists in New Zealand have been given permission to put human DNA into sheep, goats, and cattle?" Sloane repeated.

"Who gives that kind of permission? God? What can they be thinking? Cloning humans is bad enough, now they are going to cross species that have existed separately for eons?"

"Well, they have already crossed spiders with goats. When the goats are milked, there are strands in the milk that can be woven into silky light bullet proof vests for policemen. And they have crossed pigs with jelly fish and created a pig that is green clear through."

"Who needs a green pig?"

"They already use the valves of pig hearts to replace damaged human hearts because pig skin is so much like human skin. So if they do research with green pig valves they can see how the valve attaches itself and further refine the technique."

Sarah shook her head and said, "A pig does not have a soul. A jelly fish does not have a soul. A goat does not have a soul. A spider does not have a soul."

"How could we know that, Sarah? My Grandmother told me that scientists put a rat into a cage and then let a second rat loose nearby. The free rat went immediately to the caged rat and worked until he got him free. Then both rats did what appeared to be a dance of celebration. The scientists then decided to make the task more difficult by starving the free rat. They put out a dish of chocolate chips. When the free rat saw the caged rat, he ignored the food, and went straight to work to free his fellow creature. And a bird "funeral" has been observed. In a flock of birds, one died. The birds gathered around the dead one and chirped, then flew away. When they came back they all had leaves in their beaks. They laid the leaves over the dead body, stood in a circle, and quietly bent their heads down. After a few moments, they all turned and flew away. Maybe we should not be too quick to believe that only humans have souls." Why Sloane thought, did anyone need fantasy when reality was so bizarre?

Chapter Six　　THE BONNIE BANKS

"Sarah, why would someone want to kill me? I'm just a girl"

"That's why. Some of the finest scientists have attempted to confirm the existence of the Loch Ness Monster. If she exists, the value to science is immeasurable. If she doesn't, it will be a deep loss of a great myth and the end of an enormous tourist attraction for the people of Scotland. Everyone who comes to the Loch secretly wants to see Nessie. There are vast amounts of money and scientific prestige at risk. The National Geographic Society has done a special on Nessie.

The tour boats are equipped with special sonar to locate her. One man even moved to the loch to devote his life to finding her. Do you think those people want to be bested by a tiny girl from Kansas? You might as well have ridden to the loch on a broom with Toto."

"But why do they think I can prove her existence when no one else can?"

"They may be scientists but they have souls."

"Are you familiar with 'Operation Deepscan'? It happened in 1986. There were reporters, T.V. crews, and hundreds of people watching near Urquhart Castle. A helicopter was filming the operation from the air. Darrell Laurence had come to the Loch to test his sonar units. He was from Tulsa, Oklahoma, by the way. It was the largest sonar sweep of any fresh water loch. The cost was one and one half million American dollars. There were three sonar contacts. They were not fixed objects. They were not recognizable as any of the loch's known inhabitants".

Sloane didn't respond so Sarah asked, "Am I boring you with this Sloane?"

"No, no, tell me everything you know as fast as you find it out. There is something that people are overlooking and I have to figure out what it is. I'd read all 10,000 sighting reports if I thought it would help. Out of all the information, the one thing I have a problem believing is that Nessie would exit the lake and drag herself along on dry land. Her fins are not appendages like the flippers of seals and her body to fin ratio would make it impossible for her to move on dry land. She is a reptile and has no gills, only lungs. Still, the witnesses were believable. I just don't know… Read me again what they have said about her diet. I think she is a fish eating carnivore. I also think that she moves into and out of the Loch from the open sea. I need to go back to the castle. The answer is at the castle."

Sloane stood again in the royal jewels chamber. She pondered her problem as she looked at the ruby ring. She actually walked out of the room and made a circle and reentered. Then she did the same thing again. Then she ran from the room. Sarah had been looking out over the city and Sloane startled her when she ran up.

"Sarah, I know what to do. Every attempt to locate Nessie has involved action that would make her avoid the "hunters". Chasing a fish is insane. People go 'fishing not chasing.' I am going to fish for the Loch Ness Monster. I will use appropriate bait and I will catch the grandest prize the world has ever seen – a living Plesiosaur".

Chapter Seven   A FRIEND

Sloane invited Sarah to share her hotel room so Sarah could save money. Sarah had very little money and was grateful and happy to be closer to Sloane. When Sloane introduced Sarah to Maddie, Sarah quietly extended her hand and Maddie stepped right on. Animals know who they can trust. Sloane had found something that she always needed - a sister. They talked all day long. They talked all night long. The first evening when Sloane stepped out of the shower, she saw Sarah on the floor with her hands palm down on the edge of the bed. Sloane ran to her and grabbed her close. Sarah looked up startled.

"What is the matter?"

"I thought you were hurt".

"I'm saying my prayers".

"Oh, of course" murmured Sloane, embarrassed at her mistake.

"Don't you pray before you go to bed?"

"Well, no. Nobody ever taught me to do that."

"I will teach you. We'll say the Lord's prayer".

Sloane got down on her knees and held Sarah's hand in hers.

"Join in with me. Our father, who art in heaven…"

"I don't know this prayer. I don't know any prayer".

Sarah didn't want Sloane to see how surprised she was so she looked away.

"Well, then I will teach you to pray".

 So line after line, the two little Americans prayed.

"Our father who art in heaven"

"Our father who art in heaven"

 "Hallowed be thy name"

 "Hallowed be thy name"

"Thy kingdom come"

"Thy kingdom come"

"Thy will be done, on earth as it is in heaven Amen."

"Thy will be done, on earth as it is in heaven, Amen."

"Let's end with the 23rd psalm, "Yea, though I walk through the valley of the shadow of death, I shall fear no evil."

"Yea, though I walk through the valley of the shadow of death, I shall fear no evil," echoed Sloane.

"Mom, yes it's me. I'm fine. Yes. Well, Mom, I need something. Now remember, I never ask you for anything, right? Well, I need a speed boat and one thousand pounds of chocolate candy. Oh yes, and a bagpipe. Yes, I would like to learn to play it. I don't know what the balance is on my credit card. You are going to put fifty thousand dollars on the account? Mom, thanks so much. You might want to make it twice that, though. Yes, I'll play a song for you over the phone when I learn how. Oh, I'm sending Maddie home to France. She is less active and has thrown up a few times. Maybe the climate or the food doesn't agree with her. Bye, Mom."

Chapter Eight   FREEDOM

"2014, 2014," Sloane yelled as she banged into the hotel room that she and Sarah shared. Sarah bolted upright in bed and said, "Sloane, what are you talking about? What does 2014 mean?" Sloane jumped up on Sarah's bed and rattled out the news. "Sarah, in 2014, the Scottish people are going to vote whether they want to be independent of England. A vote to be free, can you imagine anything more civilized? So many have fought, so many have died for Scotland's freedom and now the Scots and the Brits are going to meet over tea and decide Scotland's future. What in the world could have prompted such an event? We must be here Sarah, you and I. Let's make a date, a pledge to be here in 2014 to celebrate the independence of this country that I love. It's so close, so close.

Think what Wallace would have thought. The British tore his living heart out of his body and then had each of his limbs tied to a horse as the horses ran in four directions. We should find his grave and tell him. Oh, I bet he doesn't have one. Well, then, let's go talk to the people in the street and hear how they feel about this momentous event. What glad news for the Scots!"

When the girls returned from their outing in Edinburgh, they were both weighed down with shopping bags. Sarah had gifts for her family, Walker cookies, Tartan plaid scarfs and wool blankets. Sloane had a bagpipe and a funny hat with ear flaps which she sat on her head to Sarah's glee. Maddie had been napping on Sloane's pillow. When she heard the girls coming back she walked to the edge of the bed to see if they had brought something for her. Sarah lovingly gave her a piece of cookie.

Settling herself down on the floor, Sloane observed, "Now, how hard can this be to play? Sarah, hand me those directions, will you?"

Sarah, handed them to Sloane, then she stepped into the bathroom.

"First, inflate the bag. That should be easy enough."

Sloane took a deep breath of air and blew into the bagpipe. The bagpipe just laid there. Again she blew and there was still no sign from the bag that anything had happened.

After four long lung blasts, the bag showed a tiny outward bulge.

"Play something, Sloane", Sarah called cheerily from the bathroom.

Sloane's face was beet red and she couldn't even speak from the exertion of trying to inflate the bag, but she blew a note.

At the sound, Maddie who had finished her cookie, ran under the bed.

"Oh good, that sounded just like the first note of "Amazing Grace", my favorite song."

When she came into the room and saw Sloane's face, Sarah picked up the directions, and said, "This may be part of the problem. It says here that after months of practice your friends will be envious of your stalwart chest and hairy thighs as you pipe in your kilt in a Scottish marching band."

"I'm supposed to stand up?" Sloane looked more than disbelieving.

"That's what it says!"

Sloane 'blapped' out a couple notes and both girls burst out in giggles when they saw that Maddie was watching and listening and seemed to be rocking back and forth and keeping time to the 'music'.

As Sarah turned to go back into the bathroom, she noticed a small bowl of marshmallows on the floor at Sloane's knee.

She yelled, "Oh no, you didn't eat any of those, did you?

Sloane jumped back and looked at the bowl.

"They're marshmallows, Sarah, what could be more innocent than a marshmallow?"

"Marshmallows are made from ground up camel hides. I'm sure you know that there is a marshmallow tree."

"Uh, no I didn't. Sarah, are you making this up?"

"No, a marshmallow is made from the root of a marshmallow tree. Many foods use ground horse hooves for gelatin but marshmallow makers use ground camel hide."

"I've never seen that on the list of ingredients."

"Of course not, who would feed their children, ground up camel hide?"

The girls climbed into bed. They lay on their sides back to back. Neither slept, but neither spoke out of regard for the other. Finally, Sloane flopped flat on her back and said,

"Sarah, have you ever had a boyfriend?"

"Why do you ask?"

"Well, I never have and I just thought it must be nice to have someone to hold you sometimes. And in bed, wouldn't it be nice to have someone warm to touch? In the United States most children don't sleep with their parents: they sleep alone and often in a different room. That's why babies wake up crying every morning. Until someone appears, they think they have been abandoned. People in South America think it is child abuse to put a baby alone in a separate room. I live alone in a separate country."

"Where does your family live, Sloane?"

"Well, there are only three of us, myself, my Grandmother, and my Mom."

My Grandmother lives in Kansas and my Mom has houses all over the world. I finally got tired of moving from one to another, so I chose to live in a chateau in France. My father gave it to me. And I convinced my mother that I was old enough to live there alone. She shouldn't have agreed. I am too young to be alone. But about that boyfriend, do you have one?"

"No, there are very few boys where I live and my mother says that love is so precious that it should be avoided as long as possible and savored deeply when one finds it. We, of course, follow the bible in all our life decisions. We do not have sex before we marry and when we marry, we marry for life. Mother says those rules are meant to make people happy and keep the family intact. I think she's right."

"I think she may be right, too! But, still…"

Chapter Nine   A PRINCE OF A GUY

"Hi, Grandma, it's me, Sloane. I need some help. You're at a thrift shop? What is that?

No, I've never been to one but I'll go sometime. The problem is this. I need a boyfriend and I've never had one and I don't know how to get one. No, I can't get one at school because I have tutors that come to the chateau. No, the tutors are all old. I don't socialize much because mom always worries that people will pretend to like me because we are so rich. Ovid, said, "You should love your equal? Yes, a rich boy wouldn't care about my money; he would have his own money. Craig's list? O.K. How about, "Wanted young prince of a guy, vast fortune, movie-star looks, and a genius I.Q, a plus". Yes, I'll let you know. The bag-pipes are a little harder to play than I thought they might be. Yes, I'll keep working. I love you too, Mom, I mean Grandmom. Bye.

Chapter Ten   A REAL PRINCE

The girls stood at the arrival gate at Edinburgh International Airport. They were there to meet Prince Hamdan, the Prince of Dubai. He had answered Sloane's Craig's List ad and was coming to meet her. The two girls couldn't have made an odder pair. Sloane was dressed in the brightest most stylish clothes and she danced and chirped like a wild parakeet. Sarah was dressed in the most somber old-fashioned clothes and bulky old shoes and was as solemn as a nun. When Hamdan stepped through the door, he could have stopped traffic. In fact, several people stopped chatting just to turn and admire him. He was the age when the softness of a woman still exists but the promise of the man to come can be sensed. He was dressed in a white dishdasha. It was obvious that he was someone who mattered. Sloane turned to Sarah, and said, "Do you think that's him?"

Sarah who was as taken by his shocking beauty as everyone else, said, "Yes, I believe it is".

Hamdan had seen Sloane's picture and he recognized her immediately. He quietly assessed her as he approached. Words from "The Song of Solomon" came to Sarah's mind. Her Mother had allowed Sarah to read the love poem of King Solomon because if the writers of the Christian Bible had chosen to include the

37

poem then who was she, Rachel Trimbath, to deprive her children of its beauty. The words of love were Sarah's favorite part of the bible.

> "Let him kiss me with the kisses of his mouth!
> For your love is better than wine,
> Your anointing oils are fragrant,
> Your name is perfume poured out;"

Hamdan extended his long well-shaped hands for Sloane to hold and said, "I am Hamdan Bin Mohammed Bin Rashid al Maktoum. My friends call me Prince Hamdan Bin Mohammed Bin Rashid al Maktoum, for short. Feel free." And as he said it, he lifted his head and broke into a smile that slashed across his smoky topaz face. Sloane's brain was washed in waves like an electric tsunami. She couldn't even speak. The Prince continued, "I am very happy to be meeting you at last. I will take a room at your hotel and then you can share the news of this grand monster adventure and we can become better acquainted. Don't bother about a taxi, my staff phoned ahead for a limo. Oh, and these are my bodyguards." Three men on each side of the prince stepped forward. Sloane stuck her hand out to introduce herself but Hamdan said, "No, don't do that. We are not so familiar with servants in my country." "Oh."

"You and I will ride in the lead car with three guards and your servant can ride in the second car with the others."

"Sarah is my friend and not a servant."

"A thousand pardons, dear lady", Hamdan said to Sarah. As he
spoke he looked at her very closely.

"I much admire the effect of your tattooing."

"This is my real color and I am an American like Sloane. I have
a very rare condition that causes my skin to be blue."

"Well, we can discuss our lives and interests at length after we're
all settled in at the hotel."

Chapter Eleven   THE TATTOO

The girls were seated side by side at the performance of The Royal Edinburgh Tattoo. They were so excited to have each other as new friends and to see the show that they held hands. They laughed and chattered like the most normal of children. Neither could remember a happier moment. The show began.

The precision drill teams marched out through the arches of Edinburgh Castle. The audience of thousands whooped and waved and cheered and laughed. There were teams from nations around the world numbering nearly a thousand performers. Along with the viewers at the castle, another million people watched on television. The show was spectacular and brought millions of dollars into Scotland.

Sarah and Sloane whooped for the dance teams, waved to the bagpipers, cheered for the military drill teams and laughed at the clowns. As Sarah smiled at a baby who was peeking at her over the shoulder of its Mother, Sloane suddenly knocked Sarah backwards out of her seat. At the same time Sloane jumped downward to her hands and knees.

She yelled, "Stay down, Sarah! Crawl and follow me!"

"Why? What is going on?"

With a nod of her head, Sloane motioned for Sarah to look back. In the seat directly in front of where Sloane had been sitting, a woman sat quietly with her head bent forward on her chest. She was dead. A woman had just been murdered in front of one million and nine thousand witnesses and Sloane was the only person who even noticed. But then, Sloane was the person who was meant to be killed.

As they crawled, Sloane saw the killer break ranks with his team and disappear into the castle.

"How did you know the killer?"

"I saw the weavers at the mill making a custom tartan for a member of the Archibald clan. The fabric in that man's kilt was missing the second yellow thread to the right of the main plaid block".

"Oh", was all Sarah could think to say.

"Sarah, get me under the castle. We have to find out who the killer is!"

"You want two unarmed girls to chase a killer?"

"If we don't, we won't be able to make a move without being paralyzed by fear!"

"I am paralyzed with fear now!"

"You are going to find out something unbelievable. When you chase people they run. It doesn't occur to them that anyone would dare to chase them who could do them no harm at all."

"Well, let's hope this killer remains unaware of what fools he's dealing with."

And down into the depths they went.

Edinburgh castle like all the great castles of the world contains underground chambers and dungeons. There were rooms for torture, rooms for prisoners and even rooms for people who were isolated because of disease. The people were left there to die. The unfortunate of Scotland had trudged these passageways for centuries and as a result the stones of the floors and especially the stairs were worn smooth. It was almost impossible to walk over the floors, let alone run. But run they did, slipping, sliding, and falling in the dark dank tunnels. The girls could hear the sounds of someone in the far distance of the corridor. Sarah began to quietly cry.

"Do you think there are rats? Oh, I hate the dark so. What if we can't find our way out?"

The sounds stopped.

"They've stopped."

"And we…" hands reached out of the dark and shoved the girls into one of the side chambers. As they fell into the room, they heard the slam of the heavy metal door and the far worse sound of a bolt being dropped into place. A lone piper played from the castle parapet as the two girls sank to the floor of the dungeon cell. In the mist and the darkness, it appeared that the piper was headless.

Sarah screamed. The sound contained all the fear and pain that had ever been felt by people who had no way out- The Jews, the Native Americans, the Rwandans. For those millions, the end had come quickly. For these two little Americans, death might not come for weeks.

"Keep screaming Sarah, scream and scream."

Sarah stopped cold.

"Why did you say that?"

"Well, when you stop, we have to start thinking of a way to get out of here and I am a bit concerned that there may not be one."

The girls reached out their arms to each other and began to laugh. They laughed and laughed and rocked in each other's arms. When they stopped, Sloane said, "As I see it, we are locked in a dungeon. No one knows we are here. We have no food and no water. We will most likely die a slow and painful death."

And off, both girls went again, into gut busting gales of laughter. They curled even tighter together like puppies on a rug.

Sloane said, "I love you Sarah Rachel Trimbath."

Sarah answered," I love you Sloane Renee Gleeson."

The girls woke to the sound of the bolt being lifted. Standing in the corridor was Prince Hamdan. Sarah rubbed her eyes because she was afraid she was dreaming. She wasn't.

The prince did not appear to be pleased to see them.

"This must stop at once. What if I had not guessed where you might be? What if you had died down here? This adventure of yours is a deadly affair and it is not something that girls should be involved in at all. Go back to the hotel and wait for me."

At his words, Sloane's dark eyes flashed, while Sarah's glowed with gratitude and admiration.

Chapter Twelve   THE LOCH

Sarah and Sloane rented a car to get to the Loch from Edinburgh. They had slipped out and not told Hamdan what they were doing. He was so domineering that they were glad to be rid of him for the day. At least Sloane was. Sarah drove because Sloane didn't know how. Sloane was reading while they drove. They were flying along the road on the edge of the Loch, when Sloane reached over and sharply turned the wheel. The car veered to the left as a huge truck came around a curve straight at them. Sarah gasped and covered her eyes with her hands.

"I forgot they drive on the left". Sloane smiled and just kept reading. They stopped at Kilmahog because Sloane started yelling, "Hammish! Hammish! I have got to see Hammish!"

In the pasture next to a small inn was a Highland bull. He was huge. His hair was red and it hung in long thick strands all over his body. Bangs hung down over his big gentle eyes. Inside the inn, it was possible to buy vegetables to feed to Hammish. Sloane with her usual verve bounced into the inn, got a bucket of chopped vegetables then walked right up to the fence and reached through it. Standing next to Hammish was a yearling named Honey. Honey was beautiful. His thick red curly fur made him look more like a bear than a calf. It was the calf that came forward to eat the fresh vegetables out of Sloane's hands. Sloane was completely in love with both, but Sarah hung back and said, "Watch out for the horns, Sloane."

Just as Sloane turned to walk back to the car, Hammish turned to watch her and his giant horns grazed the back of Sloane's head so closely that the tip of his horn actually caught a strand of her hair and flipped it into the air. She never noticed a thing. Sarah was getting used to these near misses and just smiled, shook her head, and whispered,

"Thank you, Jesus."

Both girls were hungry so they decided to get something at the sandwich shop. They both looked into their billfolds to see how much money they had. Neither of them had any at all.

"Don't worry, we'll use my credit card. Mom just put $100,000 in my account."

Sarah, laughed and said, "Well, that ought to cover it."

When they went into the shop, Sarah noticed that there was no credit card machine.

The man behind the counter told them that he could not take credit cards but if they wanted to they might be able to get cash in the little inn nearby. There was no one at the counter when the girls went in. They waited quietly for a few minutes and then yelled to let someone know they were in the building.

"Hello?"

They heard a faint creaking noise. As slow as death, the noise grew louder. Finally, an old woman in a wheelchair rolled into the room. The girls couldn't believe what they saw. The woman was like a character out of an Agatha Christie mystery novel. She was wrinkled and puckered and frumpy and absolutely grand. It could have been WWI and she was wheeling out to greet the doughboys home from the front.

"I'm setting up for the lunch crowd." There was not a person in sight.

"Do you need a room?"

"No, we need some cash."

"Cash, is it? Well, I don't have any cash."

"Couldn't you give me a cash advance on this credit card?"

"Well, I suppose I could if I knew how."

"Now, if you want to wait, Sean might be able to help. He's gone to Ben Lomond but he'll be back in a bit."

"How long?"

"Oh, about six."

"Six o'clock tonight?"

"Well, it's a bit of a drive, Miss."

"Thank you. We'll be going." And as they hurried out the door, they could hear her saying,

"Or Rorie, Rorie might be able to help."

When the girls walked past the outdoor tables they looked longingly at the plates of food that the other customers had left.

"I can't believe that you have $100,000 dollars on a credit card and we can't get anything to eat."

"Sure we can! Watch this." Sloane quickly looked over the lunch remains and picked up two plates with nearly uneaten meals on them and started walking to the car.

"We can't eat food that someone else has eaten."

Sloane was tearing the eaten edge off the sandwich and starting to eat. Sarah was watching and smelling the food. With a shrug, she reached out her hand for her share of the bounty.

The loch was not what Sloane had expected. It was a mile wide and twenty three miles long. The banks were a steep drop into cold dark water. There were no docks along its length and no boats. In fact, there were no people. Sloane had never seen a large body of water where there were no people. If a creature could survive for sixty five million years, it could very well have been in these waters. Sloane immediately knew that this forbidding place in the Scottish highlands was where she and the cryptid would meet.

The ride on the loch was more than anticlimactic. It was downright dull. But then Sloane saw the boat captain come down from the bridge to assist in a coast guard exercise. The coast guard boat was to pull up beside the tour boat and a guardsman would jump to the tour boat. The exercise was so easily accomplished that it was dull too. As the captain started to walk away, Sloane stopped him.

"Aren't you the man on the National Geographic Show about Nessie?"

"Well, yes, I am. I have lived here all my life and my only goal is to protect the creatures from harm. I have seen her twice myself.

I believe that there are as many as eighteen different creatures living in the Loch. Look at this."

He pulled his cellphone out of the pocket of his wind breaker and held it out to Sloane. "People would pay millions for this."

She looked down and on the screen she saw the form of what appeared to be two Plesiosaurs hovering in the water. Her response was, "People would kill for this." She wondered how many people had seen the captain's photograph.

Chapter Thirteen   "DOE DEN TAP TOE" (Turn off the taps.)

The Frankenstein bar was a happy place. It was decorated to look like Dr. Frankenstein's laboratory. It was very realistic. The apparatus used to raise the monster up to receive the life giving bolts of lightning was up near the ceiling. There was also a fake electric chair against the wall. Sloane couldn't wait to climb up and be electrocuted. The chair vibrated and made a funny noise. It was an interesting experience but she stepped down alive. It seemed like everybody in Edinburgh was in the bar laughing and drinking. There were thousands of people in the city because of the military tattoo. Sloane and Sarah slipped in with a group of strangers. Outside there was a late summer storm building up and it just added to the fun. The louder the thunder crashed, the louder the people in the bar talked. The lightning flashes were better than any fireworks ever. Across the room, Sloane saw the boat captain from the Loch. She nudged Sarah but Sarah didn't notice. People were packed into the bar so tightly, everybody was pressed into everybody. Sloane saw the boat captain resting against the electric chair. As a cute blonde girl laughed and stepped down into the arms of her boyfriend, the captain stepped up and into the chair. There was a deafening roar of thunder, an immediate smell of ozone and the bar went black. It was a direct lightning hit. Screams of hysterical laughter filled the air. When the generator kicked in and the lights came up there was smoke rising from the captain's head. But the captain was not in the chair. He was laying on the platform at the top of the room. His whole body was charred ash. Sloane screamed. Everybody screamed.

Chapter Fourteen   THE KISS

"Grandmother, I have an important question and I can't reach Mom. I'm not sure where she is. It's this. Do you think I'm old enough to kiss a boy? Yes, he's very nice and I like him a lot. Well, how old were you? Really, that's awfully old. I mean that's three years from now. I don't think I can wait that long. Oh, and Grandma, there's one other thing, he's a prince. Yes, he is right here with me. How did you know? O.K. and Grandma, don't tell Mom."

Hamdan took Sloane by the arm and stepped behind a building to protect her from public view. Sloane took a breath and leaned into Hamdan's arms for her first kiss. They kissed. It didn't amount to much. No bells, no whistles, what a letdown. Here she was kissing a tall, dark, handsome Arab prince on the parapets of a castle and she might as well have been filing her finger nails. Hamdan seemed very pleased with himself but Sloane had to stifle a laugh.

Chapter Fifteen   HAGGIS DINNER

Sarah and Sloane decided to have a haggis dinner. Sarah was used to food that had been shot within hours of being eaten and Sloane had experienced many unusual meals in her travels around the world, so eating a cow stomach stuffed with organ meat and oatmeal didn't strike them as an unlikely thing to do. As they walked into the restaurant, Sarah saw a display of the flags of the nations. Seeing the American flag, she said to Sloane, "Do you know the pledge of allegiance?"

No, my tutors have never been Americans and they probably just didn't think about it".

"Well, let's stand and do it here."

"Here in a restaurant?"

"Yes, no one will mind."

The young girls stood, faced the flag and put their hands over their hearts. As soon as they did, dozens of people in the restaurant stood and did the same. Then altogether, they said,

"I pledge allegiance to the flag of the United States of America and to the republic for which it stands, one nation, under God, indivisible, with liberty and justice for all."

Then all the patrons gave out with a loud round of applause.
Sarah remained standing and to a hushed room, recited Robert
Burn's "Address to a Haggis."

> Fair fa' your honest, sonsie
> face,
> Great chieftain o, the
> pudding-race!
> Aboon them a'yet tak your
> place,
> Painch, tripe, or thairm:
> Weel are ye wordy o'a
> grace
> As lang's my arm.
> The groaning trencher there
> ye fill,
> Your hurdies like a distant
> hill,
> Your pin was help to mend
> a mill
> In time of need,
> While thro' your pores the
> dews distil
> Like amber bead.
> His knife see rustic Labour
> dight,

An' cut you up wi' ready
sleight,
Trenching your gushing
entrails bright,
Like ony ditch;
And then, O what a glorious
sight,
Warm-reeking, rich!
Then horn for horn, they
stretch and strive:
Deil tak the hindmost! on
they drive,
Til a' their weel-swall'd
kytes believe
Are bent like drums;
Then auld Guidman maist
like to rive,
Bethankit! hums.

Is there that owre his
French ragout
Or olio that wad staw a
sow,
Or fricassee wad make her
spew
Wi' perfect sconner,

Looks down wi' sneering,
scornful view
On sic a dinner?
Poor devil! See him owre
his trash,
As feckles as wither's rash,
His spindle shank, a guid
whip-lash;
His nieve a nit;
Thro' blody flood <u>or</u> field to
dash,
O how unfit!
But mark the Rustic, haggis
-fed,
The trembling earth
resounds his tread.
Clap in his walie nieve a
blade,
He'll make it whissle;
An' legs an' arms, an' hands
will sned,
Like taps o' trissle.
Ye Pow'rs, wha mak
mankind your care,
And dish them out their bill
o' fare,

Auld Scotland wants nae
skinking ware
That jaups in luggies;
But, if ye wish her gratefu'
prayer
Gie her a haggis!

The people in the room roared their approval. They clapped and stomped their feet. They whistled and cheered. A handsome dark-haired young waiter strode into the room with a haggis held high on a platter. It was the ugliest edible object either of the girls had ever seen. It looked like a greasy ball of beige-gray human skin. It was tied at the top end into a knot that looked like a human navel. When the waiter drove the carving knife into the stomach with a dramatic flourish for the benefit of the cute young American girls, they took one quick sideways glance at each other and fainted dead away.

Chapter Sixteen   THE ATTACK

There were two things that Nessie had dreaded over the last months – the coming birth and the possibility of a shark attack. A shark attack was always dangerous but in her pregnant condition, Nessie was especially vulnerable. Her weight caused her to be both slower and clumsier. She was aware that she no longer existed only for herself. Two lives were at stake now. And knowing that somehow lessened Nessie's usual self-confidence. Ordinarily, Nessie would have others of her kind around her at this time. Even though Plesiosaurs tended to be solitary creatures, they joined together at the mating grounds and gathered again when the birthing time came. There were none like her at either place now. So she watched. Day after quiet day, she watched. She clung close to the sides of the loch. She had swum into the loch when she realized that she was pregnant. It was not unheard of for ocean sharks to appear in the loch, but it was rare.

The supply of fish was poor but Nessie was so close to the time of the birth that her appetite was much less than before. She had been terrified a week or two back. A giant sturgeon had caused a huge upheaval on the loch. When his shadow passed over her nest, she wasn't sure what it was. She had never in her life seen a creature so large. Several boats had been sailing the loch at the time and dozens more appeared to investigate the sighting. Nessie, always fearful of humans, dreaded the presence of the boats but soon the hubbub died down and the loch was quiet once more.

Just when she thought she was safe, it happened. He appeared like a living shard of glass slicing through the river Styx. Nessie was aware that the creature was hypnotically beautiful, but his presence meant that she was likely to die and her baby with her. She stayed absolutely still in hopes that the shark might not see her. She knew that sharks had very poor vision. But it was too late. He sensed and smelled her presence at the same moment. HE KNEW. And he turned. He swam straight toward her. He passed by her with the flourish of a bull fighter. It was a tease and she knew it. He was trying to get her to move out from the bank so he could more easily circle and snap her long neck into pieces or rip a huge bite out of her body. She would not swim into the open water. If she died, she would die where she was. He moved like a dancer in the water. Effortlessly, he turned and circled. He actually brushed against her at one point and the touch of his skin sickened her. As he brushed close, she shrank away. Twisting to the right, then the left, he could have won the battle by simply exhausting her. The fear she felt was strong enough to burst her heart in her chest. He was not large and that allowed him to be even quicker and more treacherous. She knew that he had only one weakness that she was capable of using to her advantage, his eyes.

So it was his eye that she aimed for in her attack. She only had one chance. So she took it. As he drove at her, she turned her head and bit down into his eye. She heard the orbit crack and knew she had hit the mark. He was blinded by pain. Furiously, he thrashed and tore at the space where she had been. She had moved away as soon as she heard the orbit crack and knew he no longer had any depth perception. She was safe and he was the one that would die. He turned and headed out into the open sea at the mouth of the loch. His injury was certainly not fatal but Nessie knew that he could no longer stalk and kill his prey. She sank to the bottom of the loch so heavily that anyone watching would have thought that she was the one who had died.

Chapter Seventeen   THE OTHER ATTACK

Everywhere the three friends went they were escorted by Hamdan's bodyguards. The guards were dressed exactly like him and each of them bore a marked resemblance to the prince. They could have been brothers. They were a beautiful sight and everyone they encountered stepped out of their way as they passed. Sarah felt proud and safe to be in the company of such amazing and powerful men. Sloane, however, felt suffocated. Whenever she took even a step away from the group, one of the guards was right beside her. She felt like a bird under a blanket. She had been thinking long and hard about the night that she and Sarah had spent in the terrifying dungeon. She suddenly jumped in front of Hamdan, right on the sidewalk, and stood face to face with him. The guards just stared at her.

"You locked us in the dungeon, didn't you?"

With a steady voice, Hamdan responded.

"Yes. You had to be kept safe and out of harm's way while my men hunted down the killer".

"Catch him, did they?"

"Well, no…"

"And if you locked us in, then you chose to leave us there all night?"

"Well, you needed to be taught a lesson…"

Before he could finish, Sloane drew back her arm and punched him hard in the nose. Dark red blood poured down the front of the pure white dishdasha. The guards, in a movement almost too quick to see, circled Sloane's head with a ring of snub nosed revolvers. It looked like a black halo. They said in unison, "No one touches the Prince".

To this Sloane simply stuck out her bloody forefinger and touched Hamdan on the heart.

"My name is Sloane Renee Gleeson. My name means "warrior" in Gaelic. And I'll be sure and let you know when I need a lesson from you. Understood?"

Hamdan just smiled and kept on bleeding.

Chapter Eighteen   HIS BED

Sloane stood beside Hamdan's bed. She had let herself in with the extra key. The guard who stood at the door had simply said, "Good evening Miss" when she showed up in the middle of the night. He took the key from her hand and opened the door. He did not wake the Prince. She looked down at Hamdan sleeping. His head was in profile on the pillow and he was worthy of being the face on a coin. Silk pants riding low on his hips were his only clothing. She wanted badly to touch his skin. In fact, she felt a strange urge to bite his skin. She knew that if she did, she would chew and swallow his flesh. He stirred even though she had made no move. It was probably her thoughts that spoke to him in his sleep and roused him. He opened his olive lidded eyes and said, "Sloane, is something wrong? Why are you here?"

"I am ready to have sex," she said in a clear strong voice. She waited for him to hold out his arms to her but instead he started to laugh. He laughed and he laughed.

"Well, am I that funny?"

"Yes, you are. What can you be thinking, skulking around a hotel in the night and offering yourself to me like a woman of the streets. What would your family think? You are a child, just a child and a lost child at that. Do you have any idea how exquisite, how precious you are? And do you know that when you are younger than eighteen that the interior of your body is not mature and is especially vulnerable to later cancers and diseases"? Now would you trade one night with a man, even me, and risk your health and future children?"

"Let me think about it", Sloane said and gave a crooked little smile.

"I know that in your country virginity is not as highly prized as it is in mine, but I do not rape children. Besides, I think what leads young women to early intercourse is not love or lust but loneliness. Are you lonely, Sloane?"

At this, big tears began to run down Sloane's face. Hamdan held out his arms to her and she went to him. She sobbed and sobbed. He lifted her into the bed with him, being careful to lay her on top of the covers while he lay underneath.

"Don't cry, wee bairn", he said. "You are safe here with me."

The Prince and his guards were already seated when Sarah and Sloane came down the next morning for breakfast. There was an empty space on either side of the prince. Sloane was still angry from the previous day and she led Sarah to a corner table where they could eat alone. Hamdan nodded to his men and one came and stood behind each girl's chair. Sloane groaned, nodded to Sarah and they allowed the guards to move their seats out but instead the men picked up the chairs with the girls in them and carried both chairs and girls to the Prince's table. The girls couldn't help but laugh. Hamdan said, "I apologize for my lack of judgment concerning the incident in the dungeon. To make up for it I would like you both to be my guests for a tour of Dubai. We'll leave immediately following our meal."

Sloane was furious.

"Did I hear ANYBODY agree?"

She was practically screaming.

"I've seen the world, THANK YOU VERY MUCH."

Hamdan remained calm and replied, "Ah, but you haven't seen my world."

Sloane looked at Sarah. Sarah spoke quietly without looking directly at Sloane.

"I've never seen anything."

"Oh, Sarah, I'm so sorry. How selfish of me. Of course, we will go."

Sloane visibly calmed herself and said,

"Prince Hamdan , we will be delighted to join you for a trip to your country."

She couldn't, however, erase all the sarcasm from her voice and she added, "EVER SO DELIGHTED."

Chapter Nineteen   THE MAGIC CARPET

Hamdan's private jet was one of the most beautiful things that Sloane had ever seen. The plane was a 16th birthday gift from Hamdan's father, the sheik. It was a Boeing 747. It had taken three years to design and install the interiors. It wasn't an airplane; it was a flying palace. Every item in the plane was the finest; the most expensive that money could buy. The fabrics were leather and silk wool mohair. If sterling would have been beautiful, gold was used instead. When wood was used, it was the most exotic Brazilian hardwood. The walls were all gently curved to make the interior feel more like a home and less like an airplane. The walls were decorated with vintage astronomical charts gilded with real gold. When Sarah stepped into the plane, she stumbled a little from the shock of encountering the paradise that at least for a few hours had replaced her formerly bleak existence.

There was no staff on the plane. The prince and his guests were attended by the body guards. As the plane's wheels cleared the runway, Hamdan saw that Sarah had tears in her eyes. Quickly, he unbuckled himself and hurried to her side.

"What is it Sarah? Are you ill? Are you afraid?" He took her hand.

"I've never been better."

And without a hint of irony, she said, "Thank you very much."

Sloane felt a strange unrest when Hamdan rushed to Sarah's aid. She didn't recognize it as jealousy because she had never had anyone to be jealous of or jealous over. It passed quickly.

Lunch was served on gold trays. The meal consisted of peekytoe crab tartlets and eggplant fries dusted with powdered sugar. A creamy parsnip bisque and fried oysters were followed by pork chops over stone-ground grits. There was a raspberry-pecan tart for dessert. Sparkling champagne in crystal goblets accompanied the meal. Neither girl had ever drunk alcohol before but this was a special occasion. So they glugged it down. First, Sarah began to chuckle to herself. Then Sloane joined in. Their laughter was so infectious that soon the body guards were laughing. Sarah, who was usually very quiet remembered an old joke and told it in a loud voice.

A man begged God, "Please God, let me win the lottery!"

There was no response, so again, he asked, "Please God, I am begging you, let me win the lottery." Again, nothing.

Finally, he throws himself on the ground and says, "Please God, let me win the lottery."

There is a huge clap of thunder and a voice booms down from the heavens,

"I could use a little help here. Would you mind buying a ticket?"

Sloane and Sarah actually bent over laughing. The Arabs did not understand what was funny about needing a ticket. Humor does not always translate well from one language to another but the Arabs being the gracious people that they are, laughed along anyway.

The Prince said, "I hope you do not find our lifestyle overly ostentatious. You do understand my family is billionaires".

"Yeah, mine too", bubbled Sloane.

"Mine don't have indoor toilets, but since they don't have telephones, I can't call and tell them what they're missing". And Sarah burped a loud unladylike burp.

They were approaching the coastline of Dubai. The Prince directed the girls to look out the windows. There below them was the "World". The Arabs had made islands in the shape of a map of the world. It was spectacular. Both girls squealed like children watching fireworks. Next they saw the "Palm Islands". These too were man-made islands shaped like palm trees. The fanned fingers of the palm gave water access to dozens of homes. An outer bower over the top of the palm protected the island from the ocean. Before the plane landed they were also able to see the Al Burj Arab. It is a hotel built to resemble a sail blown open by the wind. Near the top on one side is what looks like a heliport but is actually a tennis court. Sloane reached into her purse for her ringing phone. Prince Hamdan looked at her and was slightly annoyed that she was not giving her full attention to the view of his home country. So she remarked, "It's my Grandmother."

"Sloane, Sloane, I had to call you. Your Gromphadorphina portentosa is giving birth!"

"My what?"

"Maddie, your giant Madagascar Hissing Cockroach! She's having live babies. She must have been pregnant when I bought her for you. The babies are being squeezed out the back of her body in a column. The babies seem to be attached at the tail, so as they exit her body, they are forming a fan. I would show you on the phone but the picture might not be clear enough. Oh, they are beautiful. They are perfectly formed miniatures of Maddie but they're slender and white. In fact, you can almost see through them. They have black eyes and a black stripe down the back. As they unfold their antenna and break free from Maddie, they begin to instantly move about. She is letting them crawl all over her. She braced herself upside down on the side of her cage to give birth. Now she is resting on the floor of the cage. You remember that cockroaches are over 300 million years old, older by far than the dinosaurs. They have survived longer than any creature and some scientists predict that if man destroys the earth with a nuclear holocaust that cockroaches may be the only survivors. Imagine that!"

Hamdan said, "What are you looking at?"

"My pet cockroach has just had babies." She held out the phone to him.

"A cockroach? That is disgusting."

"Nothing in nature is disgusting, especially not birth."

"As you say" and he turned and looked back out the window.

Chapter Twenty   THE BIRTH

Nessie knew. She could feel a stirring deep inside her body. These weren't the quiet flutters of the past months. This felt like a separate creature from herself moving as though it wanted to be free of her. And it did. She thought she was ready, but she was very frightened. She had no fellow creature to help or comfort her. She was absolutely alone. Alone, of course, except for the creature inside her. Nessie felt waves of pain wash over her from the inside outward. As the rhythm of the pains became quicker, she felt the baby's face push out of her body. The pain, at this point, was not too intense because the baby's head and neck were small and slipped easily out of her body, but she knew what was to come. If she did not have the strength to force the baby's much larger body out of hers, they would both die. She bore down with all her strength, but nothing happened. Again, and again, she tried with no result. The baby's head and neck were long enough that Nessie could look down and see the tiny face. The little eyes were closed and the baby hung limply in the water. "No, no, no," screamed Nessie.

"She can't die. Not this baby. Not my baby."

Again, she bore down. Again, nothing. What could she do? She had no hands to drag the baby from her body. Suddenly, it occurred to her that she might be able to press the baby out by pushing her own body against a hard surface. There was a huge risk. It might tear her body open or it might crush the little one and kill her. There was no choice. Nessie moved closer to the side of the loch and pressed her body against the rocky cliff. As she gave one last giant shove and raked her body downward against the stone wall, she felt the baby break free. Nessie took only seconds to confirm that the baby had not been torn apart. The perfectly formed baby was floating seemingly lifeless in the water.

Nessie shrieked in desperation. Then she began to butt the baby. She was not getting any response and she was not gentle. She dashed the little body one way and then the other.

In a final heartrending attempt to bring the baby to life, Nessie wrapped her neck around the baby's and lifted the baby's head up into the air. Unbelievably, the baby opened its mouth and took a gulp of air. The eyes opened. IT WAS ALIVE. But this was not enough. Nessie had to get the infant to move to get its blood circulating. She had held the little one above the water to let her breathe and now she swatted the baby with her fin. Feebly at first, the baby righted herself in the water and attempted to swim. She flapped her fins awkwardly. Nessie watched the baby closely and could see it register in the baby's eyes, when the baby realized that she was the one who controlled the movement of her own body. Within an hour, the baby swam beside her mother as confidently as if she had swam in these oceans for eons not hours.

Chapter Twenty One   ARABIA – AL MUNTAHA

Hamdan handed Sloane a piece of paper and said,

"This is the itinerary for the visit, I hope it pleases you."

She looked down and read,

> DAY ONE
>
> The Palm Islands
>
> The Ferrari World Theme Park
>
> Abu Dhabi Camel Races
>
> DAY TWO
>
> Four-wheel Desert Safari
>
> Indoor skiing at Mall
>
> Dinner with Royal Family
>
> Overnight on a Dhow
>
> DAY THREE
>
> Bedouin Breakfast on the Dunes
>
> The Souks
>
> The Mosques
>
> Lunch at Palace

Sloane handed the sheet to Sarah, and smiling, asked Hamdan,

"Goodness, couldn't you think of anything else to do?"

Hamdan wrinkled his perfect brow. Sarah, ever the gentle one,

said, "It's a joke, Hamdan. Sloane is teasing you."

"Of course, of course, but if you want to stay longer, we can go out on the Royal Yacht and deep sea fish. Or we could parasail over the Arabian Gulf..."

Sloane cut him off in mid-sentence.

"I think this will be a perfect visit. Remember, we have to get back to the Loch. Nessie might make an appearance and we don't want to miss it."

The plane landed on a private air strip close to the palace. It was met by a Bentley Mulsanne with the flag of Dubai set into the front fenders. The chauffeur and attendant were dressed in a shade of bronze slightly darker than the interior of the car. Although there was no second guard car, the attendant carried an automatic machine gun in his hands. When Sarah saw this, she visibly flinched.

"We are in no danger. It is just a precaution."

"I've just never seen a gun like that. And not one carried like that. And not so close..."

"It will be okay, Sarah."

Sloane reached out and touched Sarah on the arm. At Sloane's touch, Sarah relaxed and grew silent.

The Palm Islands were even more beautiful from the ground than from the air. The chauffeur drove the blue girl, the tiny heiress, and the Prince directly there.

As they drove Sloane told Sarah the legend of Scheherezade.

"Scheherezade was the Queen of the Arabian King Shahyar. His first wife was unfaithful so the King had her killed. To avoid that ever happening again, he spent one night with a woman, and then had her killed. Scheherezade escaped death by telling the king a story every night. She told 'The story of Ali Baba' one night, and the story of 'Sinbad, the Sailor' the next night. She told the stories well but she did not tell the King the ending of the story until the next morning. And as soon as she told the end of one story, she began a new one. So for a thousand and one nights, she held the interest of her husband and king and stalled off her death."

"Did he kill her then?"

"No, during those thousand and one nights he had fallen deeply in love with her and the three babies she had given him and so she was pardoned."

Sarah craned her neck and turned from one side to the other to see. Hamdan was openly delighted by her enthusiasm. Sloane was working hard to contain her excitement because she didn't want the Prince to think that she was unsophisticated, but her heart was throbbing inside her chest with the exotic beauty that surrounded her on all sides.

As Sloane saw the billowed sail-like structure of the Al Burj Arab come into view, she suddenly choked. Hamdan, who was sitting between the two girls, reached around and began to thump her hard on the back.

"Stop. Stop. You're hitting me too hard."

"Are you okay? What made you choke?"

"Nothing. It was nothing."

She was lying. What Sloane had seen in the sail against the blue of the sky and the sea was the truth. And the truth was that Hamdan intended to keep her. And if he did, not even telling the end of the story to him at night would set her free. She wanted to vomit.

The flight to Yaz Island in Abu Dhabi was fun and fast. The young people all talked and laughed and pointed. They were having so much fun that it seemed like they were all first time visitors to the land of jewels and pomegranates. When the rearing Ferrari stallion on the largest roof in the world came into view, they all cheered. Even though the Prince had not let the park staff know about his visit, they offered to empty the park for his use. He turned to Sloane. "What is your wish?"

"Don't make anyone leave. I love to see the families. People make the park seem more like a party. I can wait in a line. It's so beautiful that I would be happy just to stand here."

"You sound like the sheik, my father. His goal is that his people, these people, be the healthiest, most educated, happiest people on the planet. Did you know that Dubai used to be a strip of barren desert and that his vision has turned it into this paradise?"

"Yes, I did know that." And off they went to play in paradise.

Sloane noticed that Abdulla, one of the prince's guards, had moved forward out of the rank of six and stayed closer to Sarah, much closer. She thought that perhaps the Prince had told him to do this, but when she saw Sarah ask Abdulla a question, he looked down at Sarah so endearingly that Sloane knew at once that the only direction he was following was from his own heart.

Sarah's eyes sparkled against the blue of her skin. Sloane had never seen her so beautiful.

Sarah was having the most fun she had ever had in her life but the spectacle of Arabia was still overwhelming to her. As the group stood staring up before the Crystal Tower, Sarah turned to Abdulla and shyly took his hand. Sloane heard her say, "I am afraid but I don't want to miss anything. This day here in paradise will never come again."

"Maybe it could, Sarah, maybe it could. But for now just watch the living people exiting the rides and know that you will survive. At the end, I will catch you if you fall."

Laughing, they got in line behind Sloane and the Prince.

The ride shot them up sixty-two meters into the air. The girls would have screamed but they couldn't get the noise out. When they reached the ground, Sarah was crying. She wouldn't tell Abdulla what was wrong, only that she needed Sloane. When Sloane stepped over, Sarah whispered that she was so scared on the ride that she wet her pants. Sarah had sadly gathered up her skirt in one hand. Sloane whispered to Hamdan, Hamdan whispered to Abdulla and Abdulla whispered to Sloane. Then the four of them proceeded to the Ferrari World Theme Park Gift Shop. Sarah stepped into the dressing room and Sloane, Hamdan, and Abdulla walked the aisles of the store. As they chose clothes for Sarah, they passed them to her through the curtain. They could hear Sarah laughing. Just as she was about to come out, Abdulla tossed a stuffed toy camel over the dressing room wall. Sarah stepped out to meet her group in a red Ferrari racing costume.

Standing there to greet her was Abdulla. He too was wearing a red Ferrari racing costume and he held a stuffed camel under his arm. When Hamdan looked at him oddly, he said,"I didn't want her to stand out in the crowd."

"Well, nobody will notice either of you now."

Sloane was cheerfully clucking over Sarah's clothes so the prince asked, "Do you want a racing costume, too?"

Sloane could no longer control her enthusiasm and she clapped her hands and jumped up and down. In moments, she too was dressed in red with the Ferrari stallion emblazoned across her chest. She strutted out of the dressing room like a runway model, turned her back, posed and flipped her dark hair. She lifted her eyes to Hamdan and smiled.

"No, not just no, NO!"

The prince described the theme park as they walked,

"The Ferrari Theme Park is covered by the single largest roof in the world. The roof is in the shape of the Ferrari symbol of a rearing stallion on the face of a shield. The park boasts the world's fastest roller coaster. There is a scale model of Italy. But nobody was listening to him.

They were hurrying from ride to ride. Too soon it would be time to leave.

Their next stop was to be the camel races.

"Do you mind if we make a short stop before we go to the camel races?"

"No, but where are we going?"

"A friend of mine is in the hospital and I would like to see how he is doing."

"What is the matter with him?"

"Well, he got in a fight with a bird and he had to have his feathers reattached."

"Who, the bird?"

"No, my friend."

"Why would they attach feathers to your friend?"

"He is a Saker falcon. They are the most expensive falcons in the world. If they lose a single feather, it affects their flight. So he is at the hospital to have a molted feather attached."

Sloane laughed and the sound was as happy and free as the chirp of a young bird.

"Do you own anything that is not the most expensive of its kind in the world?"

"Yes. Yes, I do," said Hamdan proudly. "My dog is from the animal shelter that is part of the Falcon Hospital. My Mother is a big supporter of the shelter so she let me come and choose a dog. She was grateful that I wanted a dog. One of my good friends has a pet lion. Of course, my dog is not an ordinary dog. He is worthy of his place in the royal family. I've always known fine breeding." And with that he led Sloane, Abdulla, and Sarah through the doors of the Abu Dhabi Falcon Hospital. A staff member led the visitors to one of the two hundred private air-conditioned rooms. Before they could enter, Dr. Muller appeared to greet them. Hamdan's father, His Highness Sheik Mohamed bin Zayad, is the patron of the hospital, so, of course, the hospital Director, wanted to welcome Hamdan to the facility.

"Ollie" is well on his way to a full recovery; the imping was successful. Not only are his flight feathers repaired but he passed his yearly physical."

"Ollie?" How did an Arab falcon get a name like "Ollie"?"

"He is named after the United States Ambassador Richard Olson. He even has a passport issued by the Abu Dhabi Falcon Hospital."

"Who, the Ambassador?"

"No, Ollie."

Ollie is his nickname, of course, because it is not the custom in Arab countries to give animals human names. When the young people entered the room, Ollie turned to see who had come to visit. Hamdan put on his arm guard and Ollie hopped onto Hamdan's forearm. When Hamdan raised his arm, the pupils in Sloane's eyes opened so wide that her eyes looked completely black.

The sight of the young Arab lifting the falcon on his forearm was visually exquisite. She was too young to know that uncommon things are more appealing to people or that the pupils of the eyes enlarge when a person sees something they like. She was awash in a bottomless sea of beauty and exoticism and there was no room left for reality.

Hamdan, satisfied that Ollie was well, set off for the camel races with his friends.

They quickly arrived at the royal stables. It was a concrete house surrounded by camel pens.

The house had an open area known as a "majlis" and a huge table there was heaped with dates, fresh fruit and coffee. The seating consisted of big silk floor pillows. Sloane was so excited about the camel races that she could hardly sit still long enough for Hamdan to have a cup of coffee.

All her former aloofness had disappeared and in its place was the joy and enthusiasm that was natural to her personality. She loved this strange, beautiful place and the imaginative and beautiful people who lived in it. When Hamdan said it was time to go to the track, Sloane nearly tipped over the table getting up.

Sloane loved camels and camels loved Sloane. Whenever she saw one, it would stop and look quietly at her as if he knew her. She had never felt afraid even though camels are known to have nasty tempers and will spit and bite people. The camels at the Abu Dhabi races were no different.

As Sloane walked up to the viewing area, a young camel pulled away from his trainer and dragging his tether across the sand, walked directly to her. The prince stepped in front of her but she said, "Don't worry, he is only coming to say hello."

To the wonderment of everyone watching, the young camel knelt in front of Sloane. She was charmed and reached out her hand to

pat him on the head. Hamdan barked, "Don't touch him. He is
not fully trained and he might hurt you."

Sloane touched him anyway.

The trainer had the young camel by the leash at this point. He
was annoyed that his camel had caused the Royal Party anxiety.
He tugged on the leash.

"He won't hurt him, will he?"

"It's highly unlikely. You have just been welcomed to the Abu
Dhabi camel races by an especially spectacular specimen. That
young camel is worth a half million dollars."

"Well, let the race begin."

Sloane laughed right out loud when she saw the camels lined up on the nine mile oval track.

THE JOCKEYS WERE ROBOTS.

Remote controlled robots sat on the backs of the camels. They held little riding crops. The robots were about two feet high and had torsos and little heads. At one time the camels had been ridden by children, but a law was passed that made the practice illegal and now the robots rode in their place. Oddly there was no viewing stand so Sloane stood in the desert dust along with all the other viewers and watched as the trainers dressed in helmets and padded vests moved the hundred camels into position for the race. Sloane couldn't even see her favorite. Suddenly, the race began. It was more of a stampede than a race. Camels banged into each other like "bumper cars". Some staggered. Some fell. She heard the owners yelling to the animals by phone. And then Sloane saw him.

She turned to Hamdan and said, "See him. See him right there. Oh, I wish I could yell to him."

Hamdan held out his phone.

"Go ahead, he's mine."

She was thrilled. She grabbed the phone and started shouting.

"Yella, yella, yella", which means "Fast, fast, fast".

The young camel seemed to recognize her voice. He actually moved his head as if to look for her. She stepped onto the track so that he could see her. When he did see her, he surged ahead. But

Sloane had badly misjudged the distance of the camels from where she stood. They were nearly on her when she felt someone hit her full force from behind and knock her out of the path of the thundering camels. Her favorite ran past her as she lay on the ground. He had won. It was his first race and his first win and he had done it for her. Sloane was elated as she shook the dust from her clothes and stood up. She turned to the prince but saw that he wasn't beside her. It was then that she saw his body face down in the dirt. He was unconscious and blood had soaked through the back of his "dishdasha". The "*gitra*" that had covered his black wavy hair was lying shapeless in the sand. As she reached down to him, Abdulla roared, "Don't touch him. The camels may have hit him hard enough to have broken his back."

He was furious. Sloane didn't touch Hamdan but she prayed. She prayed that she had not harmed the beautiful young creature laying at her feet. For the second time that day, the young camel pulled free of his trainer and came to where the prince lay. As he knelt, he let out a forlorn cry. At the sound, Hamdan opened his eyes. Sloane dropped to the ground. As she lay beside him, big tears ran over the curves of her face and dripped onto the sand. Hamdan smiled and said, "Don't cry wee bairn. You are safe with me."

Then he passed out again.

His guards had circled him where he lay and they stood facing outward. They swung open their human barricade when the ambulance arrived. And the ambulance was there in what seemed like seconds. The Prince was lifted onto the stretcher as carefully as if he had been made of glass rather than skin and bone. The atmosphere was grim. Abdulla watched as Sloane was lifted onto a second stretcher. She had managed to clutch Hamdan's "*gitra*" in her hand and she dragged it with her like a child drags a beloved old baby blanket. She protested,

"I'm okay. I don't need to go to the hospital."

"You're a guest of the Royal Family and you may have unknown injuries and on top of that you're slowing us down. Just do as you're told. You've done enough harm for one day."

As the ambulance doors closed, Sloane could hear the young camel crying. Even he knew that things were not as they should be.

At the hospital every test imaginable was performed on Sloane. She was x-rayed so many times that she was afraid they might have baked her like a potato. At every turn she asked,

"Is he alright? Where is he? Can I see him?"

The only response was, "As soon as we know his condition, you will be told."

Sloane's anxiety over the prince was so severe that the doctors decided to sedate her. The drugs only slowed her body. Her mind kept thrashing. She dreamed of him. Images of him flashed through her mind –Hamdan standing at the door of the cell, Hamdan kissing her at the castle, Hamdan pointing out the plane window, Hamdan, beautiful Hamdan, holding her hand at the Ferrari Park. Hamdan, Hamdan, Hamdan! When she woke hours later, she was surprised to find herself alone and without him.

Her wakened mind went wild with dread. Had he died? Would he be paralyzed? She decided that she would find him. If they would not let her see him, she would find him. If all that was left of him was a broken body, then so be it. She was going to him and no one was going to stand between them. No one. She slipped quietly out of the hospital bed onto the floor and eased across the room to the door. She thought that he would probably be in a room close by. She was right.

She peered into a dimly lit room across the hall and saw, even though the person had his back to the wall, the glossy black hair on the pillow. Just then two orderlies came wheeling a gurney down the hall. They entered the dim room and moved the patient onto the cart. Then to Sloane's horror, they pulled the sheet over the man's face. She fell straight to her knees.

"Oh God, please no. He's gone and I never told him I loved him. NO! NO! NO! This can't be!

God, give him back to me. GIVE HIM BACK! GIVE HIM BACK! GIVE HIM…"

"Sloane?"

Sloane definitely knew that the voice she heard was not God's. She slowly pivoted on her knees and looked toward the sound. Standing in the door of the next room over was Hamdan. His pearly teeth actually sparkled as he smirked at her.

"Your wish is granted. Now did you have something to tell me? If you like, you can crawl over here on your knees and tell me!"

"How long have you been there?"

"Long enough."

"I hate you. You spoiled, egotistical, Arab."

"I hate you too, you crazy American. But enough of these sweet murmurings, we can't let the staff catch us or they will keep us here even longer. Oh, and by the way, "Sloane, I love you too!" Sloane replied, "Yeah, whatever."

Two days passed and still Hamdan had not been released from the hospital. Sloane knew that she had to end the visit and return to the Loch without him. She went to the hospital fully expecting a quarrel.

Sloane screamed when she saw Hamdan. A beautiful raven-haired woman was leaning over him as he lay in the bed. Her dark hair was twined with his and it was obvious that she was kissing him. They both jumped at the sound. Actually, they all three jumped because Sloane had surprised herself by screaming. She understood now what she had felt when Hamdan paid attention to Sarah. She was jealous – crazy jealous. If he hadn't already been in a hospital bed, she'd have put him in one she thought.

"Ah Sloane, I'm glad you're here, I have someone I want you to meet."

Sloane was so heartsick, so furious, that she couldn't speak.

"I want you to meet the woman who means more to me than any other in the world."

"Then why?"

When the woman turned to look at Sloane, Sloane actually gasped. She was the most beautiful woman Sloane had ever seen.

"Isn't she exquisite? She looks like Kim Kardashian if Kim Kardashian were good-looking."

And at that, Hamdan and the magnificent Arab woman both laughed. Sloane wasn't laughing. She couldn't believe that Hamdan would be so cruel to her.

"Sloane, this is my Mother."

Hamdan's mother thought that the glittering in Sloane's eyes was because she had come to say good-bye.

"I have heard all about you, my dear, and I am so happy to meet you. Allah be praised. My son is well. And I have had the chance to meet you before you leave. You must promise to come again.

I will leave you to your good-byes. May Allah keep you safe until I see you again." That said, she floated out of the room.

Sloane collapsed onto the edge of the bed and took Hamdan's hand.

"Sloane, I know that your world is very different from mine. I also understand that you are very young and have only begun to live. Now is not the time for us, but there are two things that I want you to know. First, if you need me, I will come. No matter the place, the time, or the circumstances. I will come. I will come to you no matter what happens for the rest of my life.

Do you understand? And second, should you decide that you want to come back, then come back. Here is a gift for you."

Sloane looked down into the prince's palm and saw a ring. It was the strangest ring she had ever seen. It was a perfect replica of a Madagascar Cockroach and it was as big as one. It was completely covered in black diamonds with the exception of one white stone that sat at the back of the head where the wings met.

"This ring obligates you to nothing and me to total commitment to your well-being and happiness. In an emergency, put the ring into water and a signal will be transmitted to the palace.

We will know immediately where you are and I will leave to come to you. Remember!

And now, I need you to leave because I am sad beyond measure that you are going and I want it over quickly. I will not see you again until you want me."

Sloane started to say, "I want…" but she stopped because Abdulla had arrived to take her to the airport. There was no kiss, no touch, nothing but the prince's hollow, "until you want me".

His words were as lonely as an echo in an empty room.

On the way to the airport, Sarah and Sloane sat together in the back seat. Sarah knew how sad Sloane was to leave Hamdan, especially since he had been hurt, so she was quiet on the drive. That was easy for Sarah because unlike Sloane, she was naturally quiet. Sarah was also leaving the first man she had ever cared about and in her case the chances of ever seeing him again were nonexistent. It had come as a genuine surprise to the two young girls that what they thought would be a carefree getaway had turned into something as overwhelming as first love for both of them. Neither of them had any experience with such strong emotion and neither of them was prepared for the deep joy of young love or the deep sorrow of young loss. They were exhausted by all that had happened in such a short time.

Abdulla spoke over his shoulder to Sloane, "Sloane, I apologize for my behavior at the camel races. Protecting Hamdan is my responsibility and I let him down. It should have been me who got hit by the camel, not him. I would have willingly come to your aid but he was standing between you and me and I couldn't get past him.

You must understand, he is not only the direct heir to the throne, he is my brother."

"I'm sure you all think of the Royal Family as your family."

"No Sloane, he is my blood brother. I am Prince Abdulla of the Royal Family."

"Why didn't you tell us before?"

"He is safer if no one knows and so am I. But who better to guard the prince than his own brother?"

By that time, the limousine had arrived at the airport. Sarah and Sloane were escorted to the same plane on which they had arrived. Sloane stepped inside so that Sarah and Abdulla could say good-bye. Sarah and Abdulla were still dressed in their Ferrari racing costumes and they made a beautiful sight as they stood silhouetted against the side of the plane. Abdulla gazed at Sarah's blue face and said,

"Sarah, may I kiss you? It will probably be a long time until I see you again." She nodded.

Abdulla motioned to his guards. The guards formed a circle and raised their arms. Their flowing sleeves formed a silken arch under which Sarah and Abdulla shared their first kiss.

Unlike Sloane, Sarah's breath was taken away by the taste of Abdulla's mouth on hers.

Again she thought, "Let him kiss me with the kisses of his mouth!" The kiss was a gift from God because unknown to all but him, it was the only kiss they would ever share.

Sarah climbed the stairs to join Sloane on the plane. She stopped on the top step and turned to wave to Abdulla, then she quickly ducked inside. Abdulla watched until the plane had cleared the ground before he turned and got back into the limousine. He rode straight back to the hospital to attend to the needs of his elder brother.

As the girls settled back in their seats for the flight back to Scotland, Sarah turned to Sloane. "The plane is not magical like before is it?"

"I don't think anything will be as magical as before, ever again."

Chapter Twenty Two   THE FACE OF GOD

Ten thousand sightings and nothing for Sloane. She had spent weeks sitting on the steep bank of the loch. She had played her bagpipe and tossed out candy until she was exhausted.

It seemed that she had failed. In spite of her beauty, her youth, her money, she was a lonely child. And she was afraid. She was afraid to take Hamdan's hand and afraid not to. She was afraid that if she chose his world, she would lose her own. Nothing in her privileged life had prepared her to make the difficult decisions that she now faced. She looked toward the dark water. It would be so easy to just slip away. Then she wouldn't have to lose Sarah. She wouldn't have to decide on her religious beliefs and most frightening of all, she wouldn't have to be afraid of making the wrong choices or failing. Sloane let herself slide a little closer to the water's edge.

At that moment, a shooting star streaked across the sky. Sloane had never seen one before and she knew who was speaking. She smiled, turned her back to the water and began to slowly climb. As she turned to skim the last few pieces of candy across the loch, she blinked, closed her eyes and blinked again. There in the water, not six feet from where she sat she saw eyes. A pair of beautiful, big almond shaped eyes was looking at her. Sloane's own dark eyes filled with tears. It was her! It was the most famous Plesiosaur in the universe and she was quietly and trustingly looking at Sloane. Sloane had no camera, no witnesses, nothing. So she said, in a still small voice, "Would you like some more of this candy?"

At the moment that the candy hit the surface of the water, a second smaller pair of eyes appeared. Sloane was so excited that she could hardly breathe.

"A baby, you have a baby? Oh how wonderful is this? A baby!" Sloane couldn't have been more moved if she had seen the face of God. But then, maybe she had. Sloane stretched out her arms to Nessie. She longed to touch the magic creature. She just wanted to touch her. Nessie knew what Sloane wanted. In a terrifying move that Sloane thought might crush her, Nessie arched her giant neck up and over Sloane as Sloane stood on the bank.

In her fear, Sloane had dropped to her knees to pray. She opened her eyes to the sight of Nessie's long neck curving around her. With tear filled eyes, she stood and leaned against the creature and knew that never again would she ask anything of God. Of course, she was wrong. She would be begging within two minutes.

Suddenly, the entire coast line of the loch was lit up on both sides by torches. The torches cast eerie shadows on the walls of Urquhart Castle. For a minute Sloane couldn't think what was happening. Then she knew. They had all been spying on her and now that she had lured Nessie and her baby to the shore with music and chocolate they were here. There were hundreds of them. Sloane started scrambling up the bank, yelling,

"Dive, Nessie, Dive!"

The baby disappeared underwater but then playfully popped back up. It looked toward Sloane, then back toward its mother. Nessie sensing danger, turned away from the shore. Her baby followed close by her side. Nessie became more anxious as the crowd started to roar. A net had been suspended between two boats and Nessie swam into it in her attempt to get away and managed to wind herself tightly in the net in just a few minutes. The more she thrashed, the more the net wound around her. Sloane jumped into the water to try to cut her loose. She wrapped her arms and legs around Nessie's long elegant neck and clung to her with all the strength she had. Nessie was nearly shaking Sloane off with each crash of her huge body. Nessie whirled, she lunged, and she dove. She arched and twisted her back like a wild bronco. Her cries were like the sounds of whale songs. Nessie seemed to know intuitively that the tiny creature holding onto her neck could not stay underwater for long, so as terrified as she was, she stayed near the surface. The water was boiling from Nessie's exertions and Sloane gasped for breath each time Nessie broke the surface of the water. Sloane fought her own terror of being drowned and hacked savagely at the ropes. The crowd was a bunch of rabid dogs gone mad with excitement. They were yelling, "Kill the monster, save the child. Kill it. Kill it."

Sloane heard shots. She felt a burning pain in her leg and knew that she had been hit. Still, she fought to save the cryptid and its baby. The cold temperature of the water slowed the blood loss. Just as she felt that she was losing consciousness, she felt Nessie break free. A boat pulled up beside them. The boat was painted with the Stars and Stripes of the American flag. Twin flags flew from the rear of the boat. It must have cost at least a quarter million dollars and Sarah was at the wheel. Sarah had somehow gotten Nessie's baby on the deck of the boat. Sloane yelled, "I didn't think our boat was here, yet."

"It's not. I stole this one. Play the pipes to let Nessie know to follow." Barely able to stand or breathe, Sloane bleated out a few notes. As soon as Nessie heard the music and saw the baby on the boat, she visibly calmed. Then all four girls, Nessie, her baby, Sloane and Sarah roared down the Loch at full speed. They were trying to make it to the mouth of the Loch and to the open sea.

"Dive, dive," Sloane kept yelling to Nessie, but Nessie wouldn't let the baby out of her sight. Now, there were other boats in pursuit. Sloane knew how easily men could jump from the deck of one boat to another. She had seen it done when she took a boat ride earlier on the Loch. At the memory of it, she heard the slam of feet onto the deck. A man had managed to jump to the deck of the boat. He had an open knife in his hand and he lunged toward Nessie's baby. Sloane broke the flag off one side of the boat and used it like a lance, stabbing at the man until he was forced over the side of the boat into the dark water. Sarah yelled from the front of the boat, "You are a demon."

"No, I'm an American," Sloane responded, grinning ear to ear.
As the mouth of the Loch came in sight, Sloane hollered to Sarah to look far ahead but Sarah couldn't hear over the roaring crowd and the sound of the engine. Fishermen had made a chain of boats from one side of the Loch to the other. The boats were tied end to end with only room enough for one boat to pass through the center. Sarah finally saw the escape path. She signaled to Sloane to jump. The danger of the boats exploding was not a threat, it was absolute. Sloane jumped. Alone in the dark, cold water, Sloane was at risk of being hit and crushed to death or being chopped to pieces by the propeller blades of the boats. Almost invisible, she cried to Sarah, "Jump, jump Sarah, jump."

It was a prayer. As Sarah swerved the boat sideways into the floating chain, she scooped Nessie's baby up in her arms. The last thing Sloane saw as the boats exploded was the silhouette of the blue girl from Kentucky cradling a baby Plesiosaurus and flying through the flames.

As the water closed over Sloane's head, she didn't struggle. She didn't have the will.

She just closed her eyes and surrendered to the cold dark depths. About two feet below the surface of the water, she stopped sinking. There was something solid underneath her.

It was Nessie. Sloane was too weak to hold on. So Nessie swam slowly under Sloane and lifted her body into the life giving air. Nessie was careful not to break the surface and be seen. Slowly, slowly, she moved the dying child toward the shore and her people.

Strong hands grabbed Sloane up out of the cold water. She was not breathing.

A man roughly turned her upside down and held her by the ankles to drain the water from her lungs. He didn't bother to take her pulse. He knew she was dead. He tore the wet cold clothes off her body and tore off his own warm dry shirt and jacket. He laid her on the ground and threw himself down over her. He covered her mouth with his and began to force his breath into her body. She had turned blue. He needed electric shock paddles to start her heart beating. He remembered that newborn babies were held upside down and spanked on the butt to surprise them into taking a breath. So he quickly pulled Sloane up one more time and holding both her ankles in one of his hands, he smacked her on the rear end. She was so small that one of his hands was as big as both cheeks of her butt. She choked up more water and moved her head a tiny bit. He had her back on the ground underneath him in less than a second. Her heart was beating but the rhythm was not steady- a beat, a pause, two beats, a longer pause. He decided to stop the mouth to mouth and simply hold her against his chest so her heart would begin to match the rhythm of his own. Slowly the fluttering heart began to match his. He sang aloud, clutching her to him.

> "Amazing grace, how sweet the sound
> that saved a wretch like me,
> I once was lost but now I'm found,
> was blind but now I see.

Twas Grace that taught…
my heart to fear.
And Grace, my fears relieved.
How precious did that Grace appear…
The hour I first believed.

Through many dangers, toils and snares…
We have already come.
Twas Grace that brought us safe thus far…
and Grace will lead us home.

He rocked her gently in his arms. When the ambulance crew reached Sloane, she was laying on the ground wrapped in a man's coat and shirt. The man oddly enough had stepped away. He cast his eyes down as they approached and he was almost impossible to see in the darkness. As the ambulance doors closed, Sloane woke up screaming. He quietly smiled as the little American was driven away.

Chapter Twenty Three   SCREAMS

Nessie woke up screaming. She was back at the scene of the explosion. After pushing Sloane to the shore, she had turned immediately to try to find the body of her baby. Slashed and battered by the debris from the boats, she surfaced for one last look.

She came up too close to the burning oil and screamed as the flames scorched the right side of her face. Luckily, she was able to plunge her face down into the water before the fire got to her eye. If she lost the sight of one eye and therefore her depth perception, she could not survive. Bloody and exhausted, she swam back to her haven on the ledge.

As she reached the safety of her nest, her grief washed over her. The feelings of loss were as vast as the seas through which she swam. Over her, under her, around her, there was nothing but endless engulfing loss. She fell asleep sobbing.

As soon as she realized that it was she who was screaming, she stopped. The last thing she needed was to bring attention to herself. If her only enemies, the sharks attacked, she didn't have the strength to fight them. She wasn't sure she had the strength or the desire to live. She knew that if she chose to die that all she would have to do would be to stop eating. It would be over.

Suddenly, she heard a sound. It was a sound in her language. She was too weak to raise her head, but she opened her eyes. Hovering before her in the water was her partner from the mating grounds. He had heard her cries and had come to her. He looked for his baby and not seeing it understood the reason for her sorrow. He extended his neck and wrapped it around hers. He brushed gently over her body with his fin. He looked deep into her eyes. She was not surprised that he had come to her. After they had swum together in the mating grounds, he did not leave her side. For weeks, he fished for her and played with her. Only the lack of adequate food for two in the same area caused him to leave her side. When he left, he left slowly. He turned to see her until he disappeared in the cobalt waters.

Chapter Twenty Four   DORITO DREAMS

Grandma, yes, it's me. I know I sound strange. Grandmother, I can't do this anymore. What? Live. I can't live without Sarah. She was my best and only friend. I can't live if mother makes me leave the chateau. I can't live with Mom. It's too late. No, Neville isn't around anymore. I liked him too. Granny, do you think there is any chance that Sarah or the baby lived. Yeah, I thought not. It's not like in the movies. Do you think Nessie thought I set her up to be trapped? You're right. She knew I loved her. I loved them all. Then Sloane heard her cockroach hiss. She looked up and saw her Grandmother standing in the door of her room. She was talking to Sloane on her cell phone. Sloane laughed, slid off the bed and ran to her Grandmother. She said, "Oh Granny, what warm arms you have."
"All the better to hold you with my dear".
Sloane went limp, so dragging Sloane with her, she began to chat.
"Oh, I brought you a new book. It's about the Sasquatch. Now, if the coelacanth and the Plesiosaur have survived, it greatly increases the odds that the Sasquatch could survive too".
"How long are you staying, Grandma?"
"Forever, si'l vous plait, forever. By the by, Maddie and I have a little surprise for you. Are you ready? Close your eyes!"

Sloane turned her back. She heard the sound of what sounded like a drape being drawn.

"Okay, turn around".

Behind the drape was a wall of glass. It was the size of the entire wall of the house. On the wall was the message, "Welcome Home, Sloane!" It was spelled out by the bodies of Madagascar cockroaches.

"What is this? How did you get them to do that? Are they outside? How cool is that? Are all of them Maddie's children?"

"Well, we obviously needed more space for Maddie's children. I thought about selling them and actually sold a few but that was a hassle. And I am sad to say we had a death during shipping. So, I just decided to build a more spacious terrarium and let the family stay together".

Sloane's grandmother was enjoying telling Sloane about her work on behalf of the cockroach family.

"Now, as to the message, well, I just wrote the message in thickened honey on the inside of the terrarium wall. You'll see in a minute that when the honey is eaten up, the roaches will move away. And sure enough, when Sloane looked back at the glass, the message had changed to 'come Home'."

"Thank you, Grandmother. You're right. I did need to come home."

And that said, Sloane climbed up into her bed and pulled the luxurious shearling comforter completely over her head.

Even with her much loved Grandmother living at the chateau, Sloane did not recover from her loss. She lay in her bed for days.

She hardly moved. She hardly ate. She rarely spoke. One morning, her Grandma came into the room and said, "Get up. The Queen of England is on the phone."

Sloane had met the Queen and liked her, so she turned over and said, "What does she want?"

Her Grandmother scowled at her and held out the phone.

"Yes, hello your Majesty. How have you been? Good. You want to congratulate me for proving the existence of Nessie and saving her life. Thank you. That is very kind.

I'm to be made a Dame of the British Empire? And Sarah, posthumously? Yes, that would make me very proud. I will be there. And my family, of course. They will come too. Goodbye."

Sloane let her hand fall off the side of the bed and dropped the phone to the floor.

Before she could pull the covers back over her head, her Granny had caught them by the corner and ripped them completely off the bed.

"This stops today. You did not die. They did. Do you think you are honoring their love and friendship by wallowing in this sorrow? Get up. You have responsibilities. You are needed. Instead of always thinking about yourself, think of others. What about Sarah's family? Her Mother lost her daughter and she doesn't have your youth and privilege to see her through. She has nothing. Rise up and take care of someone else. Be who you were born to be." And she stomped out of the room. Sloane got up.

The next morning when Sloane woke up her Grandmother was standing in the door of her room. She held the muddy unicorn mask in her hand.

"Do you have any use for this? I found it down near the creek. I would like to have it if you don't want it."

"Sure, you can have it but what are you going to do with a muddy crystal horse mask?"

Holding the mask up to the light, her Grandmother answered, "These aren't crystals."

"You don't mean to tell me those are diamonds!"

"Yes, Sloane they are."

"Well, what are you going to do with a muddy diamond horse mask?"

"There are some children who have so little food that their school sends food home with them for the weekend."

"Really, where do the children live? In Africa or India?"

"No Sloane, they are little Americans. Guess how many there are?"

"I don't know. Maybe, seventy?"

"There are seven thousand in the state of Kansas, alone."

Granny had a newspaper in her other hand.

"I just saw this in the Wichita paper. A Wichita family donated 30 care packages to Enterprise Elementary School to make sure some students have adequate food for the two-week break. Thirty of the 500 students are considered homeless or chronically hungry. The school can give the students breakfast and lunch during the week, but they have no food during the weekends…"

Sloane had tears welling up in her big dark eyes as she asked, "Where do they go after school? Do they live in cars or on the street?"

"I don't know Sloane. I just don't know."

"In a country that is considered one of the world's richest?"

By this time, Sloane was tugging on her jeans.

She said, "I never knew. No one ever told me. No one. What do you think you can get for the mask?"

"I don't know."

"Look at this picture frame. It is eighteen carat gold. I don't need all this! What could you sell this for? Could you sell the chateau? Well pack your bags Auntie Em; it's time that we all got back to Oz."

Chapter Twenty Five   BACK TO OZ

It was a Wednesday when Sloane was told about the hungry little Americans and it was a Friday when she and her Grandmother boarded the plane for The United States. Neither took any luggage. Sloane had a carry-on filled with chocolate bars and her Grandma carried what looked like a gourmet lunch box. When the stewardess offered to put the lunch box in the overhead bin, Granny just shook her head and said,

"No thanks, I'll just hold the box on my lap"

"Shall I tell you about an American hero?" She said as she buckled herself into her economy class seat.

"Sure, does he have a cape?"

"Better than that, he has a conscience. His name is Warren Buffet and he is a self-made multi-billionaire. In one lifetime, he became one of the richest men in the world. I read that as a boy he would go to the race track and pick up two dollar winning tickets that no one wanted to be bothered waiting to redeem. He makes those sticky fingered superheroes in tights seem silly. He recently made a public plea for all American billionaires to donate one half of their fortunes back to the American people. And guess what, some of them did. He also found out that his secretary paid more in taxes than he did, so he proposed an increase in taxes on the wealthy. Sadly, the tax was voted down by the American congress."

"Grandmother, I've been meaning to ask you, is there any way to prevent random attacks against people?"

"Yes, killers need to stop receiving reinforcement for their behavior. Even mentally ill people know that the only way they will ever be on the front of a magazine is if they commit a vicious crime. The more famous the victim or the higher the death count, the more the trumpets blare.

This issue has already been solved by the Romans, if a Roman emperor acted inappropriately, his name was chiseled off all the monuments. When a person commits a horrible crime, no photographs should appear in the media and their name should never be said aloud again. In news articles their name should be left blank. Maybe we could call them "apls" for short – another pathetic loser. Also, why not an ad campaign that redirects their hate toward old people? I can see it now. The shooter bursts into a nursing home and the guys who fought a world war sit up in their beds, pull a gun from under the covers and give a taste of vengeance for the innocents. You do realize that all the shooters have been males with a history of confirmed mental illness. We were warned."

Suddenly in the back of the plane, there was a commotion. There was an "apl" on board and he held a knife to the throat of the young stewardess. When Sloane started to turn and get up to see what was happening, her Grandmother put her hand on top of

Sloane's head and pushed her gently but firmly down. The situation was bad and getting worse. The passengers were screaming and crying, and as the 'apl' wrestled his way toward the cockpit, he screamed, "I'm going to kill us all! Kill us! Kill us! Kill us!" Grandma began to sing,

"I am weak, but Thou art strong;

Jesus, keep me from all wrong;

"Sing Sloane, sing. Help me for the sake of God and all these people."

"I don't know the words." Sloane was stricken at not being able to help.

"Then, hold my hand and give me your strength, because I am afraid." Sloane squeezed her Grandmother's hand with all the strength she had. All the passengers who had been crying and screaming stopped and joined in the hymn.

"I'll be satisfied as long As I walk, let me walk close to Thee."

"Shut up! Stop singing! That was my mother's favorite song!"

"Join hands" yelled Granny, "We are going to sing this plane to paradise!"

Everyone on the plane joined hands – across the aisles, seat to seat, old with young.

Muslims, Jews, Christians, and Buddhists held hands and if they couldn't sing, they prayed.

Three rows ahead, a Black woman stood, and belted out the hymn. Aretha Franklin couldn't have done it any better. The passengers went quiet when her beautiful voice filled the air but they joined her for the refrain.

"Just a closer walk with Thee,

Grant it, Jesus, is my plea,

Daily walking close to Thee,

Let it be, dear Lord, let it be."

Then she sang alone,

"Through this world of toil and snares,

If I falter, Lord, who cares?

Who with me my burden shares?

None but Thee, dear Lord, none but Thee."

"When my feeble life is o'er,

Time for me will be no more

Guide me gently, safely o'er;

To Thy kingdom shore, to Thy shore."

At that point, Sloane's grandma reached into her purse and got a small bottle. When the terrorist was right beside her seat, she jumped up and threw the contents in his face. He jerked around to confront her, and released the stewardess as he did. He pulled back his arm to stab Granny but before he could get it done, Granny opened the lunch box and three hundred hissing Madagascar cockroaches whirred up out of the box. Granny had thrown honey on the gunman and the cockroaches were hissing and crawling all over his head and face. His upper body was completely black. It shimmered with the movement of the insects. He was so frightened by the roaches that he actually dropped to his knees and started to cry.

He blubbered through his tears, "Get them off me, just get them off me. Please, please, please, get them off me."

As soon as he dropped the knife, which was immediately, a handsome Frenchman tackled him to the floor of the plane. At that point, Granny opened her purse again and handed the man a coiled length of rope. She then turned to Sloane.

"Now, wasn't I telling you about one of my heroes?"

"Grandma, wait, the passengers are afraid of the cockroaches. How can I get the roaches to get back in the box?"

"They're afraid of these hissing heroes? Well, since they just saved the lives of two hundred passengers and the crew, what say we give them a little treat? Give me three of those chocolate bars."

She unwrapped the bars and laid them in the bottom of the lunch box. The roaches came scuttling back and she chuckled as they crawled over her in their hurry to get a taste of the candy.

"That tickles, guys. Wake me when we get to New York; you know I love New York."

The last cockroach to scurry into the box for her chocolate treat wore a diamond set into her forehead.

"Maddie?" Sloane asked.

"Well, I got fifty-nine thousand dollars for the mask. I hope you think that's enough. The stones were small and the clarity was off on some of them, but I figured we could still afford a little extravagance for Maddie. I had seen her admiring the ring that Hamdan gave to you. Besides, it helps me and the family recognize her more easily in an emergency. Don't let her hear this, but they really do look a lot alike."

"Surely, Grandma, you must know that cockroaches have tiny brains."

"Sometimes, Sloane, a tiny brain, a big heart and a chocolate bar are more than enough!"

Chapter Twenty Six   VOILA?

Sloane was delighted when she and her Grandmother drove up to the Hillcrest apartments.

It was a beautiful old ten story Tudor building. There was a staff of thirteen people and all of them greeted her warmly. She was after all, famous. Her delight lasted only as long as it took her to open the door to her new home. It was tiny. It was tacky. It was terrible. And there was nothing in it. She looked questioningly at her Grandmother.

"Well look around, dear! This is your new home!"

Sloane stood where she was and surveyed the whole thing. The apartment was only one thousand square feet. She peeked into the tiny kitchen, the tacky bathroom, and the terrible bedroom.

"This must be my bedroom." Sloane opened a set of double doors in the living room and a murphy bed fell out and knocked her to the floor. She looked at the hole in the wall.

"My room is a little small isn't it?"

"Oh, it will be fine. All it needs is a couple of potted plants and Voila! Oh, and a little black spray paint. We used to spray things black when they looked bad. Black hides a lot."

"Voila? We'll have a tiny, tacky, terrible black apartment with a couple of potted plants."

"Every dollar we save is a dollar we can use to help little Americans. You'll get to the point where you don't even notice your surroundings. Besides, you are an adventuress. An adventuress does not secret herself away in a house of diamonds and miss the excitement of life. By the by, have I told you that they have discovered a planet made completely of diamond? They named it 55 Cancri e. Those astronomers aren't exactly poets, now are they? Nonetheless it's up there for everybody to enjoy. And I saw a photograph of the shadow of an atom. And the Higgs Bosun, the "God" particle that holds everything in the universe together, they are getting closer to finding it. Higgs is Scottish, you know." When she turned to Sloane and saw the look on her face, her Grandmother reassured her.

"Sloane, if you find that this lifestyle makes you unhappy, we can always change back."

"Nah, I'm just a little surprised. Let's go to one of the schools and meet our new little friends."

Chapter Twenty Seven   CONCEAL AND CARRY

The school looked more like a prison than an environment created to educate and care for children. There were no plants around the building. The dirt was bare and packed hard.

Sloane and her Grandmother had to buzz to be admitted. There had been so many school shootings in America that the closed door policy was an attempt to protect the children. It was a feeble effort. When Sloane went into the classroom, the little ones jumped out of their seats and ran to her.

They wanted to touch the young heroine who was so close in age to themselves. She was stricken by the look of the children. Their hair looked like it had been cut with lawn clippers.

Their clothes were old, gray, and misshapen. Sloane had never seen poverty and these little ones were an army of the poor. Sloane couldn't even speak. Grandma however, seemed right at home.

She moved through the crush of children, patting heads, shaking hands and chatting with first one child and then another. She knelt as she walked so that her face was down close to the faces of the children. Children poured out of the rooms. The teachers could not contain them. They couldn't believe that Sloane had come to see them. Their eyes sparkled. Their voices lilted.

Today they were special and it made them happy. A little girl with faded yellow ribbons in her hair pulled at Grandma's hand and said in a shy voice, "There's a 'sojer' at the window".

"What did you say, dear?"

"A 'sojer', I saw a 'sojer'."

Grandma knew before she heard the shots. The gunman had shot his way into the school.

"Excuse me, a moment". Grandma stepped into the hall. There was a single shot. And then no sound at all. Everyone waited to see who would step through the door. Would it be the shooter or would it be Grandma? Sloane couldn't take the suspense so even though a teacher grabbed at her jacket as she passed, she got down and peeked around the corner. She saw her Grandmother and the shooter both lying on the floor!

As Sloane started to crawl to her Grandmother's side, a teacher yelled, "Be careful, he may not be dead!"

"I know but my Grandmother may be!"

As Sloane got close she saw that her Grandmother's funny old purse had a hole blown in the bottom. When she reached out and touched her, Sloane was still not sure whether she was dead or alive. Still, the children made no sound. Granny's eyes opened slowly at Sloane's touch.

"Oh, dear, I appear to have killed someone. I only got my gun license a week ago. I hope I didn't frighten the children."

"Are you shot?"

"I don't know. Am I bloody?"

Sloane heard a sound and turned to see a tiny girl with faded ribbons in her hair. She was standing in the doorway and staring at the man lying on the floor. One little finger was pointing toward him. His gun was pointed straight at Sloane. There was nothing Sloane could do. There was nothing her Grandmother could do. So Sloane said, "I shall fear no evil."

A gunshot blasted through the room. Granny had managed to aim her purse and fire again. The shooter lay dead on the floor.

"Oh no, now I have killed him. I had to but oh no, oh no!" Granny cried.

"Ma'am, you didn't kill him. I did!"

A man who looked like a cross between a giant redwood tree and George Clooney stood behind Granny.

"There's where your shot went." He pointed to the American flag. A bullet had nicked the flag pole and it drooped down. He reached over and picked it up.

"We wouldn't want it to touch the ground, now would we?"

When, Granny stood up leaning on Sloane, the children broke into wild cheers. They cheered even louder when the pizza trucks pulled up. Sloane and her Grandmother were having lunch with five hundred children at once and they were using the money from the sale of the unicorn mask to do it. To be more accurate, they had lunch with 500 students, 38 teachers, 119 parents, 10 police men, and a gerbil in a wire cage. Even the lead officer had two slices of pepperoni pizza and some breadsticks before he filled out his report.

After lunch, the policeman stopped by and whispered to Sloane, "It was your Grandmother's shot that kept those children from dying. It was mine that hit the flag pole. I lied because I knew she might not be able to live with having killed someone. You must never tell her the truth, Sloane."

"How do you know who I am?"

"The whole world knows you, miss!" And he smiled a great big "from the heart" smile.

Sloane was tired and when she got back to the apartment, she laid down to rest. Her head had not touched the pillow before she heard her Grandmother calling to her.

"Sloane Renee Gleeson, come in here!"

"Why, am I in trouble?"

"Yes, but not with me."

"Sloane, is this the picture from the Loch captain's cell phone?"

"Yes, yes it is. I could never forget that picture."

"What happened to the captain's cell phone when he died?"

"I don't know. I was so shocked by his death that I never thought to mention it to the police."

The tabloid cover slipped from Grandmother's hands to the floor.

"Who knew you were going to be at the school?"

"I'm sure it was public information. It may have even been in the newspaper."

As Sloane realized the truth, her hands began to shake.

"He came there to kill me, didn't he? Do you think he was so insane that he would have killed the children to cover up my murder? It sickens me to think that I put the children at risk by being there."

"Sloane, let's go. Hurry up. Right now. We must arm you."

"Grandmother, I can't carry a gun."

"You can, if you have to. But I think we can do better. Come on, we're going to the shopping mart."

"Where did you say we're going?"

But Sloane's Grandmother didn't answer. She was already out the door.

When they got to the store, she went straight to the garden area. She quickly put ten spray cans of wasp killer in the cart. She then went to the sporting goods area and got an archery target. Sloane didn't even bother to ask why. Sloane just stepped over to the cosmetic section and got some new eye shadow.

Back at the apartment, the two of them set up the target by the trash dumpsters and Sloane was put to work.

Grandmother explained, "This is a perfect weapon. It will disable an attacker without killing him. The spray shoots in a long concentrated pattern in order to reach wasps nests that are hidden under the eaves of houses. I want you to be as sharp a shooter with that spray can as Django ever thought of being. You may be required to protect not only yourself but others as well. You'll carry it with you at all times and at all times it must be accessible. It won't do you any good if it's in the backseat. In fact, I bet we can make you a spray can holster. You also need to get your driver's license. You can't depend on other people for transportation. You must be able to move and move quickly."

"I feel like I'm in the army".

"I wish there was time for military training for you but that is not possible. Keep shooting".

Just then, an elderly resident of the apartment building walked past and said, "Well, how thoughtful. I guess we won't have to worry about any wasps this year".

Sloane stopped to chat, but Grandma just ignored the neighbor and yelled, "Keep shooting, I'm going upstairs for two more cans."

Chapter Twenty Eight   FAMILY MATTERS

Sloane and her grandmother had just sat down to a meal of dandelion greens, tofu, fried pickles, and chocolate mousse, when grandmother said, "What would you think if we adopted Sara?"

"Sarah is dead."

"No, I mean little Sara from the school, the one with the yellow ribbons."

"What would we do with a stringy-haired little kid?"

"We'd love her."

"Isn't it enough that we have each other?"

"No, it isn't."

"WHAT? I need you. You are my mother's mother and…"

"No, I'm not."

"What are you talking about?

"I am not your mother's mother. I am your father's mother."

"How could I not know that? You mean that you are Claude's mother?"

"Claude is not your father. My son is your father."

"O.K. So WHO is my father? Juan, Neville, Justin Bieber?"

"It really doesn't matter. He's dead."

"Dead? Dead? What did he die from?"

"He was murdered."

"Oh come on, first you tell me that you are not my mother's
mother and then you tell me that my father, whoever he was,
was murdered. And then when we finally get to be together you
tell me that you want to bring a stranger into the family."
"Maybe two."
"TWO WHAT?"
"Strangers. I've been thinking about asking Brad out on a date."

"The cop?"

"Yes, he was so cute. Of course, I'll have to pretend to believe that silly tale that he shot the shooter. He couldn't have; the angle was way off." And with that she popped a pickle in her mouth.

"Grandmother, he couldn't have been fifty and how old are you, seventy?"

"You're right. I've given that serious thought and I've decided that he's not too old for me."

"I can't cope with all this at one time."

"Sloane Renee, you act like someone who knows nothing of life, family, or reality. Oh, I guess you don't, do you? Well, it is normal in a family for a Grandmother to have a Grand-father at her side, and for a young girl to have a sister. How could you possibly think that I could have a happy life just sitting and looking at you? Do not misunderstand, I adore you. You are my dead son born again. Listen to what Shake-speare had to say,

> When forty winters shall besiege thy brow,
> And dig deep trenches in thy beauty's field,
> Thy youth's proud livery so gazed on now,
> Will be a totter'd weed of small worth held:
> Then being asked, where all thy beauty lies,
> Where all the treasure of thy lusty days;
> To say, within thy own deep sunken eyes,
> Were an all-eating shame, and thriftless praise.

How much more praise deserv'd thy beauty's use'
If thou couldst answer "This fair child of mine
Shall sum my count and make my old excuse,
Proving his beauty by succession thine.
    This were to be new made when thou art old,
    And see thy blood warm when thou feel'st it cold.

"Do you know how close you are to your final flight to adulthood? I may be standing here talking to the Queen of Dubai, or I may be talking to the adventuress who will prove or disprove the existence of all the cryptids in the world but I am not standing here talking to a child who needs me. They called from the school. Sara's Dad died in prison. If we don't take her, she will be put in an orphanage. I need you to think over my question. Do we want a family or do you want me to be alone and little Sara to be alone like you have been alone all your life?
"Why would anybody want to kill my Dad?" (You see not even a heroine can behave admirably all the time).

Chapter Twenty Nine   OVER THE POND

The time had come for Sloane to revisit Great Britain. She had been given honorary citizenship because only British citizens can be named Peers of the Realm. She was ready.

The ceremony was to take place at Westminster Abbey. In recent times, the rite had been simplified. The Queen simply pinned the medal on the chest of the recipient in a quiet ceremony. Sloane was to join the ranks of world famous artists, statesmen, and adventurers. She was thrilled to be so honored. And for her ceremony, the old traditions were all to be in place. She would walk the aisle of Westminster and the Queen would raise a sword, lower the flat side of the blade onto her shoulder and name her Dame Gleeson. The entire world had gone love crazy for the tiny American girl who had called up a monster from the depths and risked her life to protect it.

Her costume for the occasion was intended to reflect her American pride. The designer was the American icon, Ralph Lifshitz Lauren. The gown was very blue, very plain, and very fitted. Across her upper body was a sash that echoed the red and white stripes of the American flag. Her earrings were blue sapphire stars.

Sloane was not intimidated but she wanted to be alone in the abbey before the event. She needed to steel herself against the grief she was afraid might well up and overcome her. She had visited Westminster before, but never had she felt the sense of awe that she felt now. As she walked through the Abbey she saw the grave marker for Darwin and she was deeply moved. It worried her that she had to step on grave stones as she walked, so she tried to tiptoe around the edges. It was next to impossible to do. Finally, a guard spoke to her and said,

"Miss, there is only one marker that you must avoid stepping on and that is the one for the Unknown Soldier. It is over by the west entry. And may I add, I hope you are enjoying your time in England, Sloane Renee Gleeson, Gaelic warrior."

"How do you know who I am?"

"The whole world knows you, Miss."

On the day of the ceremony, she awoke happy and well. She and her Grandmother were sharing a room and it made Sloane smile when she opened her eyes and saw someone who loved her. She didn't know whether her Mother would be at the ceremony. Her Mother had been on safari in South Africa when the news was announced and she had called to tell Sloane how proud she was. She did not come back. Sloane and her Grandmother rode in a white limousine with American flags flying on the front fenders. Along the route, thousands of people, waved and cheered as they passed. At one point, her Grandmother opened her purse and got out what looked like a little Asian cricket cage. Inside sat Sloane's pet cockroach. She hissed. Her Grandmother opened the cage and Sloane squealed with delight. Quick as could be, the cockroach scurried over to Sloane, ran up the front of her dress and settled into her dark hair. As they reached the Abbey, Sloane's grandmother leaned over and said, "You sum my count, and make my old excuse."

Sloane was escorted into the Abbey by Prince Harry and Prince William. The photographers were in a frenzy. The well-wishers brought back memories of the crowd at the Loch but Sloane took a deep breath and remembered her responsibilities to herself, her country, her friends, and her family. She straightened her back. She was taken to a small anteroom to wait until the ceremony was to begin. She spoke aloud to Sarah, "Well, beloved sister, we are not locked in a dungeon today."

"We're ready."

It was Prince Harry. It had been decided that he and William would walk behind Sloane and stand beside her during the ceremony. This again was not according to custom, but was to prevent Sloane from being completely alone in front of the hundreds of elite guests who filled the Abbey. Sloane began the walk. It was hard not to wave or to gawk at the guests. She saw the President and First Lady Michelle. She saw Sir Elton John and David Beckham. She saw Lady Gaga. As she looked up the long aisle, she saw the Queen. Sloane smiled and the Queen smiled back. Sloane looked toward where her family was seated. And there sitting next to her Grandmother was Sloane's own beautiful Mother, Circe. To her right sat Prince Hamdan. When the Arab prince saw Sloane look his way, he took his index finger and pointed it at his heart. Three more steps and Sloane was standing before the Queen. The Queen's voice rang out against the stone walls of Westminster.

"We are gathered here today to welcome Sloane Renee Gleeson into the ranks of the peers of England. She is a heroine of the first order. This tiny American called forth the mighty Plesiosaur, a creature that has been protected by British law since 1912 and risked her life to protect it. As we all know, Sarah Rachel Trimbath lost her life in the same effort. Sarah Rachel Trimbath is to be named a Dame of the British Empire, posthumously. Please kneel".

Prince William handed the sword to his grandmother.

"Sloane Renee Gleeson and Sarah Rachel Trimbath by the powers entrusted to me as the reigning Monarch of England, I hereby name you Dame Sloane Renee Gleeson and Dame Sarah Rachel Trimbath. The empire and the world will be forever in your debt". The bells of Westminster began to peal. The guests in the abbey rose in unison. As Sloane turned to walk back down the aisle, she looked toward her family. It was then that she saw Sarah standing in the shadow. At the sight, the tiny Gaelic warrior slipped into unconsciousness and melted to the floor. All that could be seen at the feet of the Queen was a puddle of red, white, and blue fabric and the glint from a blue sapphire star that shone through a swirl of dark hair.

Chapter Thirty   THE FOLDING OF THE WINGS

Sloane woke up screaming. Her Grandmother was instantly at her side; holding her and stroking her shining dark hair.

"Shush, shush, don't be afraid. You are not alone. I am with you. Oh, stop child, please stop. You are breaking my heart."

"Grandmother, I can't bear it that Sarah is alone and in the water. We didn't even get her body back to bury. And I keep dreaming of her face. I did see her at Westminster. I didn't imagine it. I saw her. Grandmother, do you believe in ghosts?"

"Sloane, I believe in everything!"

"She is trying to communicate with me. I have to go back."

Sloane's grandmother was quiet for a moment, and then she said, "Very well. We'll go back. We'll go back and say good-bye to Sarah and then maybe she and you can both rest. But Sloane, don't forget that Sarah was deeply religious. She is sitting at the feet of Jesus, and baby Nessie is there too. You are the one who is forsaken. She feels no pain, no loneliness- those are the concerns of the living."

Sloane wanted to invite Rachel, Sarah's mother, to go to Scotland for Sarah's funeral.

She knew that she must do this in person. So she went to the hill country and began her walk to Sarah's home. When Sloane got close to the cabin where Sarah's mother lived, her pace slowed to a stand-still. If it hadn't been for Sloane, Sarah would still be alive. If Sarah's mother hated Sloane, Sloane wasn't sure she could go on. Sloane thought she saw the curtain move at the window, but she couldn't be sure. She sank down in the dirt of the road. There was nothing left of Sloane. Then a blue face appeared above her. Rachel's face was back-lit by the sun and she seemed as beautiful to Sloane as a renaissance angel. She smiled as she gathered Sloane in her arms.

"My Sloane, my Sloane. My second daughter, you have come at last. Safe in my arms, you are here at last. Well, truly, the Lord giveth and the Lord taketh away. Welcome to our home, lovely girl. Welcome home."

And together they wept.

After they had cried themselves dry and the road to mud, Rachel rose and carried Sloane into the cabin. She laid her down in Sarah's bed and sat in a rocking chair beside her. When Sloane opened her eyes, it was dawn of the next day and Rachel still sat by her side. Rachel said, "Sarah sent me a letter from Scotland. Would you like to read it?"

"Yes, please."

> "Dearest Mother,
> Thank you for letting me make this trip. I know how worried you were that something might happen to me. Well, it did. The world is beautiful and I have made good and loving friends. Sloane is my dearest sister and we each have added much to the life of the oth-

er. She is wealthy beyond what we could imagine but lonely, while I am poor but enriched by my family and love of God. She held back nothing from me and in return, I introduced her to the Lord. Now, I have seen the world's treasures and she, with the love of Jesus, will never be alone again.

P.S. I have a boyfriend. His name is Abdulla and even though he is not a Christian, he is devout in his beliefs. He is also very handsome. Not even Sloane knows that he is the blood brother of Hamdan. That means that if we were to marry that Sloane and I would live in Dubai together as I am sure she will one day be Hamdan's queen. And of course, you could join us and live there too. I have never known such happiness. I will tell you more when I get home. I am looking forward to seeing you Mother.

Your loving daughter,

Sarah

Sloane refolded the letter and handed it back to Rachel.

"Mrs. Trimbath, I am here to invite you to come with me to Scotland. We are going to have a funeral service for Sarah at the Loch."

"Sloane, when I received the news from the Scottish police that Sarah had died, I went up on the mountain and said my goodbye to her. I have never been out of this valley and the thought of going so far frightens me."

"Oh, please come. I need to know that you don't hate me. I would gladly have died in her place. Please, believe me."

"I do believe you. It was her time, not yours. I love you because she loved you. And I love you because I am a mother without a daughter and you are a daughter without…" Rachel couldn't bring herself to finish the sentence.

"If you will help me to not be afraid, I will come with you."

Their bargain was sealed with a kiss and a hug.

Hamdan was standing alone on the bank of the Loch when Sloane arrived. The wind whipped his exotic robes against his perfectly

muscled body. He looked like a young god. When he saw Sloane, he stretched his arms out to her. His eyes were dark with tears as were hers. She ran to him and laughed as he wrapped her in his arms. They were such an exquisite pair that they could easily have spread their wings and soared to Mount Ararat. Sloane realized with a shock that the way they looked now was the scene she had seen on the side of the Burj. Hamdan took a step back to look at her, then, he kissed her deeply. The kiss was that of a man, and it was meant for a woman not a child. In one instant Sloane understood passion. Her blood flowed hot in her veins and her face was flushed. Hamdan knew that she was moved.

"I understand that while I could not keep you safe, your cockroach did."

Sloane gently pulled the collar of her blouse to the side and there sat Maddie in the curve of her throat.

"I have been wrong about so many things." He lifted his hand to Maddie and she gingerly stepped onto it.

"Diamond wearing cockroaches, blue people, monsters? How is it that a tiny American girl can lead a life as interesting as an Arab prince?" Sloane arched one of her bird-wing eyebrows at him.

"Oh, alright, MORE interesting than the life of an Arab prince." That said, Hamdan lifted Maddie to the white *"gitra"* he wore. She sat there like an onyx brooch with a diamond highlight and if cockroaches can feel pride, she felt it.

A platform had been built in front of Urquhart castle for the funeral. Seated on the platform were Sloane, Rachel, Hamdan,

Abdulla, Sloane's Grandmother, and the Queen of England. Next to Hamdan, little Sara sat on Brad's lap. Her hair was tied up with bright new yellow ribbons.

She held Sloane's stuffed camel in her arms. Hundreds of people had gathered on the banks of the loch and the loch itself was filled with boats. A group of pipers stood to Sloane's right and at a nod from Sloane, the pipers, played "Amazing Grace." She stood and played with them.

Abdulla and Sloane stepped up to the microphone. Abdulla began to read an Islamic funeral prayer. Even though he was a member of one of the most powerful dynasties on earth, he was a broken hearted boy who could do nothing but surrender the young girl he loved to her fate.

> "O God, forgive our living and our dead, those who are present among us and those who are Absent, our young and our old, our males and our females. O God, whoever you keep alive, keep him alive in Islam, and whoever you cause to die, cause him to die with faith. Do not deprive us of the reward and do not cause us to go astray after this. O God, forgive him and have mercy on him, keep him safe and sound and forgive him, honour his rest and ease his entrance; wash him with water and snow and hail, and cleanse him of sin as a white garment is cleansed of dirt. O God, give him a home better than his home and a family better than his family. O God, admit him to Paradise and protect him from the torment of the grave and the torment of Hell-fire; make his grave spacious and fill it with light."

As Abdulla concluded the prayer of his people for Sarah, he felt someone at his side. It was Sarah's mother, Rachel. Rachel put her arms around Abdulla and hugged him hard. She put one hand into his shining dark hair and brought his head down to her shoulder. She knew. She hugged the man who would have been the father of her grandchildren. Rachel, who had no education, no life experience, no significance in the world knew that all people, all cultures, all religions were good. She was one of the richest, happiest people on earth. She welcomed the prayers of all for her beloved daughter. She and Abdulla sat down side by side.

Sloane began to read. She could only say the first word before she was choked by a sob. She stood quietly for a moment, then turned and walked to Abdulla. She handed him the pages and in the shadow of Urquhart Castle, Abdulla's strong voice rang out,

> Peace my heart, let the time for the parting be sweet.
> Let it not be a death but completeness.
> Let love melt into memory and pain into songs.
> Let the flight through the sky end in the folding of the wings over the nest.
> Let the last touch of your hands be gentle like the flower of night.
> Stand still, O Beautiful End, for a moment, and say your last words in silence.
> I bow to you and hold up my lamp to light you on your way.

The mourners looked to the darkening sky at the end of the poem and saw there the words, "I SHALL FEAR NO EVIL." The sun sank below the horizon and at the moment of total darkness, lights on the boats flashed on, lanterns were lit, torches were set afire and there was a blaze on the loch that shone high into the night sky to light Sarah on her way.

ABOUT THE AUTHOR

Dr. Susan Phibbs Cecil is a Behavioral Science Professor at Butler Community College. She is a world traveler (32 trips, so far), an internationally exhibited artist, and an art collector. She is a member of Mensa and is the recipient of numerous awards such as a Kennedy Center Certificate for her Contribution to Art Education. She has three children and three grandchildren. She loves the world, her family, her students, and she loves ALL YOU BANDITS.

ABOUT THE ILLUSTRATOR

Peter Dorman Johnson is a painter and printmaker. He holds an M.F.A. from Wichita State University. Formerly a gallery owner, he now works alongside his wife, the painter Marilyn Johnson, in their studio in the Flint Hills of southeast Kansas. Peter and Marilyn are the parents of six sons.